Rescued by the Mountain Guide

Angel's Peak Steamy Instalove Power Dynamic Novels

Book Two

Ellie Masters

Master of Romantic Suspense

JEM Publishing

DEDICATION

This book is dedicated to my one and only—my amazing and wonderful husband.

Without your care and support, my writing would not have made it this far.

You pushed me when I needed to be pushed.

You supported me when I felt discouraged.

You believed in me when I didn't believe in myself.

If it weren't for you, this book never would have come to life.

ALSO BY ELLIE MASTERS

The LIGHTER SIDE

Ellie Masters is the lighter side of the Jet & Ellie Masters writing duo! You will find Contemporary Romance, Military Romance, Romantic Suspense, Billionaire Romance, and Rock Star Romance in Ellie's Works.

YOU CAN FIND ELLIE'S BOOKS HERE:

ELLIEMASTERS.COM/BOOKS

SUGGESTED READING ORDER

START HERE

Rockstar Romance

The Angel Fire Rock Romance Series

EACH BOOK IN THIS SERIES CAN BE READ AS A STANDALONE AND IS ABOUT A DIFFERENT COUPLE WITH AN HEA. IT IS RECOMMENDED THEY ARE READ IN ORDER.

Heart's Insanity

Ashes to New

Heart's Desire

Heart's Collide

Hearts Divided

Hearts Entwined

Forest's FALL

Hearts The Last Beat

CONTINUE HERE...

Rescuing Malia

Rescuing Ally

Delta Team (Coming Soon)

Rescuing Ember

Rescuing Aria

STANDALONES IN THE GUARDIAN HOSTAGE RESCUE SERIES YOU CAN READ ANYTIME

Military Romance

Guardian Personal Protection Specialists

Sybil's Protector

Lyra's Protector

Angel Peak Steamy Instalove Series

(Small Town Power Dynamics)

By Ellie Masters

EACH BOOK IN THIS SERIES CAN BE READ AS A STANDALONE AND IS ABOUT A DIFFERENT COUPLE WITH AN HEA.

SNOWED IN WITH THE MOUNTAIN DOCTOR

Rescued by the Mountain Guide

Stranded with the Resort Owner

Matched with the Small-Town Chef

Trapped with the Forest Ranger

Snowbound with the Vineyard Owner

Reunited with the Hometown Hero

Colliding with the Coffee Shop Owner

The One I Want Series

(Small Town, Military Heroes)

Ellie Masters writing as L.A. Warren

Vendel Rising: a Science Fiction Serialized Novel

If you enjoyed this book by Ellie Masters, the LIGHTER SIDE of the Jet & Ellie writing duo, and aren't afraid of edgier writing, you might enjoy reading BDSM themed books written by Jet, the DARKER SIDE of the Masters' Writing Team.

The DARKER SIDE

Jet Masters is the darker side of the Jet & Ellie writing duo!

Romantic Suspense

Changing Roles Series:

THIS SERIES MUST BE READ IN ORDER.

Command Me

Control Me

Collar Me

Embracing FATE

Seizing FATE

Accepting FATE

HOT READS

A STANDALONE NOVEL.

Down the Rabbit Hole

Light BDSM Romance

The Ties that Bind

EACH BOOK IN THIS SERIES CAN BE READ AS A STANDALONE AND IS ABOUT A DIFFERENT COUPLE WITH AN HEA.

Alexa

Penny

Michelle

Ivy

HOT READS

Becoming His Series

THIS SERIES MUST BE READ IN ORDER.

The Ballet

Learning to Breathe

Becoming His

Dark Captive Romance

A STANDALONE NOVEL.

She's MINE

To My Readers

This book is a work of fiction. It does not exist in the real world and should not be construed as reality. As in most romantic fiction, I've taken liberties. I've compressed the romance into a sliver of time. I've allowed these characters to develop strong bonds of trust over a matter of days.

This does not happen in real life where you, my amazing readers, live. Take more time in your romance and learn who you're giving a piece of your heart to. I urge you to move with caution. Always protect yourself.

Blurb

He warned her not to go up the mountain. Now she'll never want to come down. One blizzard. One bed. No boundaries. She came to conquer the Rockies. He came to rescue the reckless.

Cloe Matthews is chasing the story of her career—a feature on hidden mountain gems for a top magazine. But when a blizzard turns her solo hike into a life-threatening disaster, she finds herself clinging to a cliff and praying for a miracle.

Enter Jackson Hart: Angel's Peak's best mountain guide, brooding, brutally hot, and not exactly thrilled to be saving a stranded "city girl" who ignored every warning.

Forced to shelter together in his remote mountain cabin, the storm outside is nothing compared to the one brewing between them. The heat they try to ignore quickly becomes combustible—and impossible to contain.

She's all fire and ambition.

He's all control and restraint.

But when survival means surrender, can either of them hold the line?

One room. One cot. Zero chance of staying untouched.

This mountain man is about to ruin her... and rewrite everything she thought she wanted.

Angel's Peak

Angel's Peak

CHAPTER 1

WARNING SIGNS

THE QUAINT SIGN FOR ANGEL'S PEAK EMERGES through my windshield, wooden and hand-carved, dusted with a light powder of early morning snow. A bubble of excitement rises in my chest—finally, after three years of writing cookie-cutter travel pieces about overpriced tourist traps, I've landed an assignment with actual substance.

My editor's words replay in my mind: *"Make this good, Matthews, and we'll talk about that staff position."* The validation I've craved since joining Pathfinder Magazine dangles just within reach.

I ease my rental car into the small town center, where buildings with timber facades and pitched roofs line a single main street. Christmas lights still twinkle in shop windows despite January being well underway. The kind of place where everyone knows everyone—exactly what my urban readers will eat up.

My growling stomach guides me to Maggie's Diner, a chrome-and-red establishment that could have been plucked straight from the 1950s. The bell above the door announces my arrival, and heads turn—outsiders clearly a novelty here. The warmth inside fogs my glasses instantly, carrying scents of coffee, bacon, and something sweet.

A waitress with silver-streaked hair pulled into a neat bun approaches as I slide into a booth. Her name tag reads "Darlene," and smile lines frame kind eyes.

"Coffee, honey?" She brandishes a pot without waiting for my answer.

"Please. And whatever that amazing smell is." I unwrap my scarf, savoring the heat against my chilled cheeks.

"Cinnamon rolls. Just out of the oven." Darlene pours the steaming coffee into a mug with mountains etched into the ceramic. "Haven't seen you around before."

"Just got in. I'm writing an article about hidden gems in the Rockies." I pull out my notebook, eager to start collecting details. "Places tourists overlook but shouldn't."

Darlene's eyebrows lift. "Well, you picked a risky time to visit. Storm's coming in tonight. Big one, by the looks of the sky."

"I checked the forecast before driving up. It said we'd just get a dusting." My phone sits on the table, and the weather app suggests nothing more than light snow.

"Those forecasts are set for the valley." A man's gruff voice carries from the counter. He's beefy, with a salt-and-pepper beard and a park ranger uniform. "Up here, weather's got a mind of its own. Pete's station's picking up a serious system moving faster than expected."

"Serious as in...?" I try to keep my tone casual.

"Serious as in twenty inches and sixty-mile winds by midnight." Darlene slides a massive cinnamon roll in front of me, steam carrying its spicy sweetness upward. "You might want to gather what you need today and hunker down at your hotel tonight."

Disappointment curdles in my stomach. I only have four days here, and my deadline looms next week. A lost day means trouble.

"I'll be careful." I drizzle icing over the roll, watching it melt into the swirls. "But I really need to get some preliminary shots of the trails today. Any recommendations for something with a great view that won't take too long?"

The diner grows oddly quiet.

"Lookout Point's your best bet," the ranger finally offers. "Three miles up, well-marked trail. But be back down by two, no exceptions."

"Absolutely." I scribble the name in my notebook. Three miles is nothing. With my new hiking boots and the trail guide, I should be fine. The worried glances exchanged around me seem excessive.

City girl stereotyping at its finest.

The bell above the door jingles, and the atmosphere shifts instantly. The temperature in the room seems to drop several degrees despite the cozy warmth. Curious, I turn slightly in my booth.

A man stands in the doorway, tall and broad-shouldered, with dark hair dusted with snow and a jawline that could cut glass. His presence fills the small diner, though he hasn't said a word. Clad in well-worn hiking gear and a heavy jacket, he stomps snow from his boots with precision.

No one speaks. Even Darlene hesitates before approaching him.

"Morning, Jackson. The usual?" Her voice carries forced cheerfulness.

He nods once, sharp and efficient, scanning the room with eyes as blue and cold as glacial ice. When his gaze lands briefly on me—the obvious outsider—something like irritation flickers across his features.

I straighten my spine instinctively. Something about his dismissive assessment rankles.

"Coffee to go, Darlene. And two of those." He points to my cinnamon roll.

That voice. Low and rough, like it's been dragged over gravel and whiskey, and somehow still smoother than sin. It slides down my spine in a slow, deliberate shiver, curling around something deep in my belly I wasn't expecting.

I blink, trying to shake the reaction, but it's already there —lodged behind my ribs, warm and unwelcome.

The man's presence is... magnetic in the most inconvenient way. Every inch of him screams backwoods danger— silent, brooding, and built like he could wrestle a bear into submission just for the exercise. He doesn't look at me again, but I feel the weight of that single glance like a brand on my skin.

"Storm's moving fast," he says. "Everyone ready?"

It's not a question. It's a warning.

My fingers tighten around the warm ceramic of my coffee mug, and I suddenly feel every beat of my pulse against the porcelain.

Who the hell is this man?

And why the hell did my heart just skip?

The diner hums with quiet energy now, every local tuned to him like a barometer for whatever's coming. He doesn't wear a badge, but he might as well. Authority clings to him like the snow melting off his shoulders—quiet, cold, absolute.

"Got a writer staying at Mabel's place," the ranger says, nodding in my direction.

Like I'm not sitting three feet away. Like I'm part of the furniture.

Jackson's glacier-blue eyes flick to me again, this time assessing. Not the once-over kind of look I'm used to from men in bars or conferences. This one is colder. Calculating. Like he's measuring my worth and already finding it lacking.

It's not curiosity. Not appreciation.

It's dismissal.

And it hits all wrong.

I'm used to double-takes and lingering smiles. Free drinks sent down the bar. The slow lean-in of male attention, half-flirt, half-dare. Men trip over themselves to hold doors, start conversations, ask for a photo—anything to keep me in their orbit a little longer.

But this man?

He looks right through me.

Like I'm a risk assessment, not a person. Like I'm a problem he's already solving in his head.

My spine stiffens. Heat flares in my chest—part insult, part challenge. I know what I look like. I've used it to open doors, charm sources, and get interviews others can't. It's not vanity —it's strategy.

But he doesn't care.

Worse—he's already decided I don't matter.

And that, more than the storm or the sudden shift in the room's energy, pisses me right the fuck off.

"Writer?" he asks, still not addressing me.

"Heading to Lookout Point," the ranger replies, as easy as you please.

I set my coffee down with a little too much force.

"Not today." Jackson's tone is final, like a slammed door. His gaze slices back to the ranger, ignoring me entirely. "She's not—"

He stops, lips pressing into a hard line. Whatever he was about to say, he swallows it.

But I've heard enough.

She's not...?

Not what? Not capable? Not local? Not worth speaking to directly?

I bristle, heat rising in my chest.

"Excuse me," I cut in, my voice sharp enough to draw a few looks. "But if we're going to decide where I can and can't go, maybe you could include me in the conversation?"

The two men look at me then, but it's Jackson who holds my gaze.

Calm.

Controlled.

Completely unfazed by my anger.

"That storm hits, and you're out past the ridge; no one's coming to get you," he says. "So yeah. I'm telling you *not* today."

I rise from the booth, pulse hammering. "And I'm telling you, I'm not some clueless city girl who wandered in with a camera and bad boots. I've done this before."

His gaze drops to my boots—perfectly broken-in waterproof hikers, thank you very much—then back to my face, still unreadable.

"Good to know," he says simply, like that changes nothing.

And maybe it doesn't.

But I'm not about to be dismissed like some reckless tourist who needs saving.

Not by this man.

Not by anyone.

"Whatever you were told about the weather is outdated." His attention fixes entirely on me now, intense and piercing. "Storm's accelerated. If you want pictures, take them from your hotel window."

"And who are you to tell me what to do?" My cheeks burn. The condescension in his tone ignites something defiant in me.

A strange hush falls over the diner again.

"Jackson Hart. Mountain rescue." He doesn't elaborate further, already turning toward the door. "Stay in town today, city girl."

With that, he's gone, leaving nothing but cold air and an impression of absolute authority in his wake.

"Don't take it personally," Darlene whispers, refilling my coffee. "That's just Jackson. Knows these mountains better than he knows himself."

The ranger nods. "Best guide in three states. If he says the trail's closed, it's closed."

Frustration simmers beneath my skin. My entire career hangs on this article, and some mountain man with a superiority complex isn't going to derail it.

"Who does he think he is?" I mutter, tearing off a piece of cinnamon roll with more force than necessary.

The diner goes oddly quiet again. An older woman at the counter clears her throat. "He's earned the right. Lost his fiancée up there three years back. Climbing accident. Hasn't been the same since."

"Emma," someone else adds softly. "Sweet girl. He was leading a group when it happened."

"That's terrible." My irritation deflates slightly, replaced by an unwelcome twinge of sympathy.

"Terrible enough that when Jackson Hart says to stay off the mountain..." Darlene raises her eyebrows meaningfully. "You *stay* off the mountain."

"I understand." The words taste false even as I speak them. I'm on a deadline, which means I'm headed up that trail. Besides, the ranger said I could, as long as I'm back by two.

Ten minutes later, I'm in my rental car, driving toward the trailhead for Lookout Point rather than to the lodge, where I have a room for the next four days. My conscience prickles, but my ambition speaks louder.

Three miles up, quick photos, three miles down. I'll be back before noon. *Before* the storm hits. The sky above still shows patches of blue between gathering clouds, and the wind hasn't picked up significantly.

As I lock the car and consult the trail map, my new hiking boots crunch on fresh snow. Clear markers lead the way, and I've downloaded the route to my phone. This Jackson person is probably just being overly cautious—understandable given his history, but I'm not some helpless tourist. I grew up hiking in Vermont. Different terrain, sure, but the principles remain the same.

The first mile passes easily, the trail winding through pine trees heavy with snow. My camera captures the pristine wilderness, perfect for the "untouched beauty" angle my article needs. The silence wraps around me like a blanket, broken only by the soft padding of my boots and occasional birdsong.

By the second mile, the wind picks up, whipping loose strands of hair across my face. The trees thin out, exposing me to the elements more directly. Clouds have swallowed the remaining blue sky, turning everything a flat, ominous gray. Second thoughts nag at me, but I'm more than halfway there. Turning back now would waste the entire trip up.

Just push forward. Get the shots. Head back down.

How bad can it get?

The trail steepens, and my breathing grows labored. The altitude—something I hadn't adequately accounted for—makes every step more taxing than expected.

A gust of wind nearly knocks me sideways, and the first heavy snowflakes begin to fall. Not the gentle, picturesque flakes from earlier, but hard, driving pellets that sting my cheeks and gather rapidly on my jacket.

Maybe this wasn't such a good idea.

The thought barely forms when the trail marker ahead disappears behind a sudden curtain of white. The wind howls now, disorienting me as visibility drops dramatically. My phone's GPS flickers, the signal wavering.

Stay calm. Follow your tracks back.

I turn, heart thumping painfully against my ribs, only to find my footprints already filling with fresh snow. The path I took up has vanished—Gone—replaced by an indistinguishable blanket of white.

Panic rises, sharp and metallic in my throat. The storm wasn't supposed to hit for hours. Jackson was right—it's accelerated beyond all predictions. And I, in my stubborn pride, ignored every warning.

Think, Cloe. Think.

The trail map shows a shortcut—a narrow path that cuts across the switchbacks, potentially shaving precious minutes off my descent. I squint through the thickening snow, spotting the faint indentation of the cutoff winding sharply downhill. Steeper. Narrower. Less traveled.

But it slices the mountain like a blade. Right now, speed matters more than caution.

The moment my boot hits the incline, the terrain shifts underfoot. Not packed trail—loose shale, dusted with snow, hiding patches of slick ice beneath. My heel slips. I pinwheel an arm for balance, my heart thudding as gravel skitters down the slope, vanishing into the mist below.

A low branch whips across my cheek as I push forward, stinging cold against skin already raw from the wind. The path narrows again, no more than a goat track now, and it hugs tight to a drop-off that disappears into swirling white. My boots crunch down, but the snow gives unevenly—some spots soft and shallow, others concealing frozen rock that sends me skidding sideways until I catch myself against a pine trunk, bark scraping my palm.

Every step demands full attention and commitment. One

wrong move and this shortcut stops being faster and starts being fatal.

My foot slips.

Time slows.

One moment, I'm upright; the next, I'm sliding uncontrollably down the steep incline, snow and rocks tumbling with me. My trail pack tears away, disappearing into the whiteness. I claw desperately for purchase, fingernails scraping against hidden ice until my body slams against something solid —a narrow outcropping of rock that halts my descent.

Pain lances through my left ankle. The ledge beneath me can't be more than three feet wide, dropping away into swirling white nothingness below. Above me, the path I slid from seems impossibly distant.

Shit.

I'm trapped.

My hands, bare after losing my gloves in the fall, grow numb against the freezing rock. The storm envelops me completely now, visibility reduced to mere feet. No one knows where I am. No one is coming. The realization sinks into my bones, colder than the snow accumulating on my shoulders.

"Help!" My voice sounds pathetically small against the howling wind. "Somebody help!"

Minutes blur into what might be an hour. My body trembles uncontrollably, and my fingers lose sensation entirely. Consciousness begins to waver, darkness edging into my vision.

This is how it ends.

Not with the career breakthrough I dreamed of, but frozen on a mountainside, a cautionary tale for other ambitious fools.

My eyelids grow heavy, the deadly comfort of sleep beckoning.

Through increasingly unfocused vision, something moves

in the blizzard above me. A hallucination, surely—my oxygen-deprived brain conjuring hope where none exists.

But then it comes again—a flash of color against the white.

And then, impossibly—a rope drops beside me, slicing through the thick white haze like judgment itself, the end swinging in the violent wind before thudding against the ground, inches from my frozen hand.

I stare at it for one beat, and then I know with absolute certainty who my rescuer is.

Of course.

Of course, it's *him*.

Jackson fucking Hart.

Heat surges beneath my cold-soaked skin—not from relief but fury. Embarrassment. Shame that tastes like blood in the back of my throat.

He was right.

About the storm.

About the trail.

But not about me.

I'm not some reckless idiot. I've hiked harder terrain than this. I've summited peaks he's probably only flown over. But none of that matters now—not when I'm half-sliding down a mountain, and he's throwing me a lifeline.

He's going to think I'm exactly what he warned me not to be—just another foolish, unprepared city girl who wandered too far past the guardrails.

My pride screams at me not to take it.

But my fingers close around the rope—frozen, stiff, furious.

Because survival comes first.

And proving Jackson Hart wrong will have to wait.

Angel's Peak

Chapter 2

Rescued

The rope sways in the howling wind, my salvation only inches from my numb fingers. Through the blinding snow, a dark shape materializes above—a man anchored against the blizzard's fury.

"Grab it! Now!" The voice cuts through the storm, commanding and unmistakable.

Jackson fucking Hart.

My frozen muscles scream in protest as I reach for the lifeline. The rough fibers scrape against my raw palms, but the pain barely registers against the burning cold. My fingers, clumsy and stiff, struggle to grip.

"I can't—" The words catch in my throat, raspy from the frigid air.

"You can." His voice leaves no room for weakness. "Wrap it around your wrist. Do it now."

Something in his tone bypasses my frozen brain, triggering instinctive obedience. My right hand clutches the rope, winding it once, twice around my wrist. The rope bites into my skin, an anchor to consciousness.

Jackson's face appears at the ledge's edge, snow crusting his dark beard and eyebrows. His expression is carved from granite—all sharp angles and controlled fury.

"Harness coming down." His voice cuts through the wind, impersonal and clipped. A moment later, a climbing harness thuds into the snow beside me. "Step into it. Legs first, then secure it around your waist."

I reach for it with hands that barely work, fingers stinging as blood rushes back in painful little stabs. The nylon is stiff and unyielding.

"I don't know how—"

"Figure it out." His reply is flat. Cold as the snow crusting in my eyelashes. "Or freeze. Your choice."

Rage flares hot and sudden—cutting through the fear like a blade.

Figure it out?

I am figuring it out. I've been figuring it out since the moment I set foot on this godforsaken trail, long before his smug, mountain-man ass showed up to play hero. I grit my teeth, biting back the words I want to hurl at him.

The harness is deceptively simple. Two leg loops. Waist belt. Click. Secure.

Three fumbles. Five curses under my breath. Then it's done.

"Done!" I shout, sharper than necessary.

Let him hear the fury in my voice. Let him know I may need help getting off this mountain—but I sure as shit don't need him talking to me like I'm helpless.

Without warning, the rope goes taut, and my body lifts slightly. Terror spikes through me as my feet lose contact with the ledge.

"Hold on to the rope. Keep your feet against the rock face." Jackson's instructions carry down from above. "Walk your feet up as I pull."

The ascent is agonizing. My ankle throbs with each movement, muscles trembling with cold and exertion. Ice-encrusted rock scrapes against my chest and thighs as I'm hauled upward, inch by painful inch. The blizzard batters my body, threatening to slam me back against the cliff face.

After what seems like hours but must be minutes, strong hands grip the harness at my waist, hauling me over the edge onto more solid ground. My body collapses into the snow, my lungs burning with each gasping breath.

No time for recovery. Jackson kneels beside me, his face inches from mine, eyes blazing with controlled rage. Snow collects on his dark hair and the shoulders of his heavy-duty parka.

"Can you stand?" The question sounds more like a command.

"I think so." My ankle protests as he helps me upright, his grip firm through my jacket.

"Sprained?" His gloved hands probe my ankle through my boot, assessing.

I wince. "Maybe."

He unzips his pack with quick, practiced motions—no hesitation, no wasted effort. An elastic bandage appears in his gloved hands, already half-unrolled.

Then he drops to one knee before me and reaches for my boot.

"Hey—what the hell do you think you're doing?" I snap, jerking back instinctively, pain lancing through my ankle. "You can't just—"

His eyes snap to mine. Glacier-blue. Unblinking.

"I'm treating your injury," he bites out, voice low and edged with steel. "Unless you'd rather I leave it to swell until you can't walk at all?"

My mouth opens. Closes. The glare he levels at me could freeze the rest of the mountain.

Without waiting for another protest, he returns to the

task, unlacing my boot with sharp, decisive movements. Cold air hits my ankle like a slap as he peels the boot away and carefully rolls down my sock.

"This needs compression. Hold still," he orders, wrapping the bandage steadily.

I do. But not because he told me to.

Because I can't stop staring at him. That jaw—tight with tension. Those hands—strong, sure, capable—moving with the kind of confidence that comes from doing this a hundred times before. No hesitation. No gentleness, either. Just efficient, competent control

And God help me, it's hot.

My skin burns, even in the cold. The rush of adrenaline from the fall is long gone, replaced by something heavier. Thicker. A slow, pulsing heat that coils low and dangerous.

Damn it.

Jackson fucking Hart is right again. And I hate that what I'm feeling right now—under his hands, under his command—isn't just gratitude. It's not just survival.

It's desire.

Sharp. Immediate. Completely inappropriate.

I hate that he makes me feel this way. Hate that I want to snap at him one second and climb him like a tree the next.

Judging by the way his jaw ticks as he finishes the wrap, he knows it.

Which somehow makes it worse.

His touch is surprisingly gentle as he wraps the bandage around my ankle, but his words cut like ice. "You were told explicitly not to come up here."

"I thought I had time before—"

"You thought wrong." He secures the bandage and roughly replaces my boot. "You risked your life, and now mine."

"I didn't ask you to come after me." Heat rushes to my cheeks despite the freezing temperature.

"So I should have left you to die?" His eyes snap to mine, piercing blue against the white landscape.

The bluntness of his words steals my retort. Death. It hadn't seemed real until now—the true consequence of my stubborn pride.

Jackson stands, assessing our surroundings. The storm has intensified, snow swirling around us in violent gusts. Visibility extends barely ten feet in any direction.

"We can't make it down." His expression darkens. "Night's coming. Temperature's dropping. We need shelter."

"My car's at the trailhead," I offer, clinging to the illusion of an easy escape.

A short, humorless laugh escapes him. "Three miles in whiteout conditions, with your ankle? We'd be finding your frozen body in spring." He gestures up the slope. "My shelter's half a mile up. It's our only option."

The reality of the situation crashes over me. We're trapped on the mountain together—this man who clearly despises me and the woman whose recklessness vindicates every negative assumption he's made about me.

"Can you walk?"

He's already moving, already coiling the rope, like rescuing stranded hikers is just another chore on his list.

"Yes." The word snaps out sharper than intended—my pride lashing before my common sense can catch up.

His eyes flick to my wrapped ankle. One brow arches. Jackson Hart doesn't argue; he just *knows* I'm lying. He shrugs into his pack like it weighs nothing, then steps in close. Too close. His arm slides around my waist before I can protest— solid, unyielding, warm.

"Lean on me. And try to keep up."

I want to shove him away. I want to prove I can do this on

my own. But the moment I take a step, white-hot pain slices up my leg, and I suck in a gasp. Pride be damned—I'd collapse without him.

I hate this.

I hate how strong he is. How steady. How the arm around my waist doesn't just support me—it grounds me. Every step is agony, but worse than the pain is the heat simmering low in my belly. Not from exertion. Not from adrenaline.

From him.

From the way his body moves beside mine—powerful, efficient, always in control. From the way he never looks back, just trusts I'll fall in line. From the quiet competence in every step, every adjustment, and every flex of muscle under that worn jacket.

It's infuriating, and completely unfair.

Because I should be cursing this storm. My ankle. This entire detour.

Instead, I'm cursing how I keep glancing up at his jawline. The way my skin burns where his hand grips my hip. The way, for a single humiliating heartbeat, I wonder what that hand would feel like lower.

And I hate that I want him.

Jackson fucking Hart.

The human glacier. Stoic, bossy, maddening.

And under all of that—goddamn irresistible.

I grit my teeth and lean harder into him. Not because I need to. Not entirely.

Because I want to remember how this feels—just long enough to make myself forget.

The journey up the mountain is a blur of pain and cold. Each step sends shards of agony through my ankle, but Jackson's firm support never wavers. The storm rages around us, transforming the landscape into an alien white wasteland.

Wind slices through my inadequate clothing, finding every seam and gap.

"Almost there." Jackson's voice at my ear barely penetrates the howling gale.

A dark shape materializes through the curtain of snow—a small structure nestled against the mountainside, almost invisible against the surrounding rocks. Relief floods through me, overwhelming even the pain.

Jackson guides me to a heavy wooden door, unbolting it with one hand while supporting my weight with the other. It swings open, and he ushers me inside before the wind can steal our precious body heat.

Darkness envelops us, broken only by the faint gray light filtering through a single small window. The air inside smells of wood, dust, and something metallic—a stark contrast to the sterile cold outside.

"Stay put." Jackson releases me, and I sag against the wall.

The scratch of a match breaks the silence, and warm light blooms as he lights an old-fashioned lantern. The shelter reveals itself: a single room, perhaps fifteen feet square, with stone walls and a wooden floor. A small woodstove occupies one corner, a narrow cot against the opposite wall. Metal shelves hold supplies—canned food, bottles of water, medical supplies, and tools. A table and two chairs stand in the center, utilitarian and worn.

"Not the Ritz," Jackson mutters, moving toward the woodstove. He kneels, arranging kindling and logs with efficient movements.

"It's..." Words fail me. Primitive? Lifesaving? A prison with my least favorite person as warden?

"Shelter." He strikes another match, igniting the kindling. "Which is more than you had twenty minutes ago."

Another barb I can't refute. The fire catches, casting flickering light across the small space. Jackson moves around the shelter with the familiarity of habit, checking supplies, adjusting the ventilation on the stove, and lighting another lantern.

"Sit." He points to one of the chairs, his tone leaving no room for argument. "Ankle elevated."

My body moves before my pride can argue, collapsing into the seat like I've been cut loose. The second I stop moving, the exhaustion hits—sharp, relentless, total. The adrenaline that kept me upright seeps out of my pores, leaving me limp and shaking.

Jackson kneels in front of me again, reaching for the laces of my boot.

He pauses, fingers hovering.

"You gonna bite my head off again if I touch you?"

I glare down at him, my lips pressed tight. "Depends. You planning on barking another order?"

His gaze lifts slowly. That icy-blue stare holds mine, unwavering. "Only if you do something stupid."

My mouth opens—but nothing comes out.

Because he's right.

Again.

"Fine," I mutter. "Proceed, Dr. Doom."

The edge of his mouth twitches—just barely—but he doesn't respond. Just sets to work, unlacing my boot with calm, practiced efficiency. There's nothing sensual in the movement, no hesitation. Just steady, clinical care. And still— still—my breath catches.

"This needs ice," he says, inspecting the swelling. "Ironically, we've got plenty."

He rises and steps to the door, scooping snow into a clean cloth with the same precision he used coiling the rope, binding my ankle, and apparently, pissing me off in the most maddening, effective way possible.

"Here." He places the makeshift ice pack on my ankle, then

hands me a bottle of water and two pills. "Ibuprofen. For inflammation."

"Thank you." The words taste strange on my tongue—gratitude mixed with humiliation.

He doesn't acknowledge my thanks, already turning away to retrieve a hand-crank radio from a shelf.

"Angel's Peak Search and Rescue, this is Hart." He speaks into the device after several cranks. "I have the writer. We're at my upper shelter. Conditions zero visibility. Remaining in place until storm passes. Over."

Static crackles before a voice responds: "Copy that, Hart. Writer's vehicle located at Lookout trailhead. Storm expected forty-eight hours minimum. Confirm supplies adequate. Over."

"Supplies adequate. Will radio at 0800 tomorrow. Hart out." He sets the radio aside and turns to me, his expression unreadable in the dancing firelight.

The magnitude of our situation settles over me. Forty-eight hours. Trapped in this tiny space with a man who clearly wishes I never set foot in his town.

"I'm sorry," I offer, the words inadequate even to my ears.

Jackson's eyebrows lift slightly—the first hint of surprise he's shown. "Sorry you didn't listen, or sorry you got caught?"

Heat flashes across my cheeks. "Sorry you had to risk your life because of my mistake."

He studies me for a long moment, as if assessing the sincerity of my apology. "You're not the first tourist to under-estimate these mountains." His voice holds a weariness that suggests he's had this conversation before, perhaps with less fortunate outcomes.

"I'm not a tourist." The defense rises automatically. "I'm a writer. Researching."

"Tourist, writer, researcher—doesn't matter what you call yourself. The mountain doesn't care about your job title when you're freezing to death on a cliff face." He moves to the shelves, taking inventory of canned goods. "You hungry?"

The abrupt change of subject catches me off guard. My stomach answers before my mouth can, growling audibly.

The corner of Jackson's mouth twitches—not quite a smile, but a crack in his stone façade. "I'll take that as a yes."

He selects a can, opening it with a manual can opener before emptying the contents into a small pot. In a few minutes, the rich aroma of beef stew fills the small space as he places it on the woodstove.

"The generator's for emergencies only." He nods toward a small machine in the corner. "Heat, light, and communication are the priorities. We have enough fuel for about eight hours total. We use it sparingly."

"So... no microwave, I'm guessing?" The weak attempt at humor falls flat.

Jackson doesn't bother responding. Instead, he retrieves two metal bowls and spoons from a shelf. He stirs the stew occasionally as it heats, his movements economical and practiced.

The silence stretches between us, broken only by the crackling fire and howling wind outside. Questions burn in my mind—about him, this shelter, the fiancée mentioned in hushed tones at the diner. But his closed expression discourages conversation.

"Why did you come after me?" The question escapes before I can reconsider.

Jackson's shoulders stiffen almost imperceptibly. "Your rental car was at the trailhead after I explicitly closed the trail. Simple deduction."

"That's not what I asked."

He turns, fixing me with that penetrating blue gaze. "What would you have me do? Leave you out there?"

"Some might have. Especially someone who warned me not to go in the first place."

A muscle twitches in his jaw. "I don't need the validation of being right at the cost of someone's life."

His words hang between us, heavy with implications I can't fully decipher. Before I can probe further, he divides the stew between two bowls, handing one to me along with a spoon.

The first bite floods my mouth with warmth and flavor—nothing fancy, but nourishing and exactly what my cold-ravaged body needs. We eat in silence, the stew warming me from the inside.

Jackson finishes first, setting his bowl aside. "We need to establish some ground rules. We're going to be here at least two days. Possibly three, depending on how the storm plays out."

"Rules?" The word bristles against my independent nature.

"Rule one: Conservation. Water, food, fuel—all limited resources. Nothing gets wasted." He ticks off points on his fingers. "Rule two: Communication. The radio stays cranked. If something happens to me, you need to be able to call for help."

The casual mention of his potential incapacitation sends an unexpected chill through me.

"Rule three: This is a survival situation, not a hotel stay. You do what I say when I say it without argument. This isn't about authority—it's about keeping us both alive."

My natural instinct to challenge authority rises, but reason prevails. He knows this mountain, this shelter, this situation better than I ever could.

"Seems reasonable." I set my empty bowl aside.

Jackson studies me, skepticism evident in his expression.

"You sure? You haven't exactly demonstrated a talent for following instructions so far."

The barb hits its mark. "I made one mistake—"

"A mistake that nearly killed you," he interrupts, voice sharp. "And could still kill both of us if this storm lasts longer than predicted."

The reality of our predicament settles over me like a physical weight. My ankle throbs, a persistent reminder of my vulnerability.

Jackson sighs, running a hand through his snow-dampened hair. In the firelight, exhaustion shows clearly on his face —lines around his eyes and mouth that weren't visible in the harsh daylight. For the first time, I see beyond the mountain man stereotype to the human beneath.

"You should rest." He nods toward the cot. "I'll take the first watch on the fire."

"Watch? As in... taking turns sleeping?" The single narrow cot suddenly looms large in my awareness.

"One bed, two people, sub-zero temperatures outside. You do the math." His tone is flat, practical, already turning away to arrange logs beside the stove like the conversation's over.

But it's not.

Not for me.

Two days. One bed. And him. A man who finds me more nuisance than necessity, whose every word bristles with judgment... and yet whose very presence has my skin tightening beneath layers of fleece.

Jackson moves to check the window, his broad shoulders stretching the fabric of his jacket, the collar framing the powerful line of his neck. Frost creeps across the pane, but I swear it's warmer in here now—because my body's suddenly burning.

In the low light, his profile is distractingly perfect. That jaw—sharpened by stubble and attitude. That nose—straight, uncompromising. And his mouth... firm and unsmiling, but shaped with a sculptor's precision. The kind of mouth that should have no business making my thighs clench just from existing.

But it does.

And now my brain, despite the trauma and pain and freezing cold, is conjuring up images I absolutely do not need. Those lips—on my throat. My shoulder. Lower. His hands pressing me down, anchoring. That mouth taking, claiming, ruining.

Damn it.

He turns slightly, and I jerk my gaze away like I haven't just mentally undressed the man who dragged me off a mountain. But it's too late—my pulse is already thundering, my cheeks flushed. Not from the cold.

No, this heat is all Jackson fucking Hart. And I hate that I want more of it.

"Storm's getting worse." His voice cuts through my inappropriate observation. "We made it just in time."

As if punctuating his statement, the wind rises to a shriek, rattling the shelter's walls. A draft snakes across the floor, curling around my injured ankle.

Jackson meets my gaze, something unspoken passing between us. "Get some sleep. Tomorrow won't be any easier."

The cot beckons, my body crying out for rest. But as I rise awkwardly, favoring my good ankle, a new awareness settles over me. This mountain man saved my life despite every reason not to. And now we're bound together in this primitive shelter, dependent on each other for survival.

The most dangerous part of this situation might not be the blizzard raging outside, but the unexpected feelings beginning to stir within these close confines—feelings I have absolutely no business entertaining toward the man whose life I've endangered through my own stubborn pride.

Angel's Peak

CHAPTER 3

FRICTION

LIGHT FILTERS THROUGH THE FROST-COVERED window, barely distinguishable from last night's darkness. The blizzard continues its assault, snow piling against the shelter's walls with audible weight. I blink awake on the narrow cot, disoriented before memories flood back—the fall, the rescue, Jackson.

My ankle throbs beneath the blankets, a persistent reminder of yesterday's foolishness. Despite the woodstove's glow, the shelter feels colder than last night, suggesting Jackson let it burn down while I slept.

He sits at the small table, methodically cleaning what appears to be a disassembled radio. His broad shoulders hunch over the delicate work, and his strong fingers are surprisingly nimble with the tiny components. He hasn't noticed I'm awake yet, allowing me a moment to observe him unguarded.

In the gray morning light, Jackson Hart is no less intimidating than he was yesterday. His jaw is set in concentration, dark hair falls across his forehead, and those capable hands move with certainty. He looks like he belongs here—rugged, self-sufficient, part of the mountain itself.

I shift slightly, and his head snaps up, that intense blue gaze pinning me in place.

"Storm's worse." No good morning, no pleasantries. "Another system merged with this one overnight."

"How long?" My voice comes out raspy from sleep and the shelter's dry air.

"Three days, minimum."

The words land like stones in my stomach. Three days in this tiny space with this unyielding man.

Jackson rises from the table, moving to the woodstove to add another log. "Generator's acting up. Need to conserve what little juice we have."

I push myself upright, wincing as my ankle protests. "What needs to be done?"

Something like surprise flickers across his features—perhaps he expected complaints rather than offers of assistance.

"Inventory." He nods toward the shelves. "Food, water, medical supplies. Need to know exactly what we're working with."

It's a task suited for my injured state, requiring minimal movement. I appreciate that he hasn't mentioned my limitations. Swinging my legs carefully off the cot, I test my weight gingerly on the injured ankle. Better than yesterday, but nowhere near healed.

"Here." Jackson appears beside me with a makeshift cane —a sturdy branch cut to height, the bark stripped away to reveal smooth wood beneath. "Made it last night."

The unexpectedly thoughtful gesture catches me off-guard. "Thank you."

He shrugs, already turning away, a man uncomfortable with gratitude. "Coffee's ready. Not the fancy stuff you're probably used to."

"I'm not actually that high-maintenance." The defensive words escape before I can stop them.

Jackson's eyebrow lifts slightly, skepticism evident without a single word spoken.

"Despite what you clearly think of me." I hobble toward the table where a metal mug steams with black coffee.

"What I think doesn't matter." He focuses on the generator in the corner, a squat, battered machine that looks older than both of us combined. "What matters is getting through the next few days alive."

The coffee tastes surprisingly good—strong and hot, exactly what my body craves. Jackson kneels beside the generator, tools spread around him in precise order. He works quickly, adjusting, tightening, and testing.

"Running rough." He speaks more to himself than to me. "Need to clean the fuel line again."

I turn my attention to the task assigned: cataloging our supplies. The shelves hold more than I initially thought—canned goods, dried foods, water bottles, medical supplies, extra clothing, and emergency equipment. Each item is placed with logical precision, nothing wasted, nothing frivolous.

"Twelve cans of stew, eight of beans, four of corn, six packets of jerky, ten protein bars," I call out, making mental notes. "Twenty liters of water, plus whatever snow we can melt."

"That's enough. Even if we're stuck here for a week." He doesn't look up from the generator.

"You always keep this place so well-stocked?"

"Always prepared. Mountains don't forgive lack of preparation." The words carry weight beyond their literal meaning.

Working methodically across the shelves, I reach a section that seems more personal—books, a compass, a few tools, and —partially concealed behind a manual on alpine survival—a small framed photograph.

Curiosity pulls my hand toward it before consideration can stop me. The simple wooden frame holds a sun-faded image of a woman standing triumphantly on a mountain summit. Her smile radiates even through the weathered photo —bright, joyful, alive. Long auburn hair escapes from beneath a climbing helmet, whipping in what must be substantial wind. Strong, capable-looking, with a grace even the still image can't disguise.

Beautiful.

"Put that back." Jackson's voice cuts through the silence, sharp as a blade.

Startled, I nearly drop the frame. Jackson stands a few feet away, his expression thunderous, body rigid with tension.

"I was just—"

"Put. It. Back." Each word is precise and controlled, but with undercurrents of something dangerous.

I put the photo exactly as I found it, partially hidden from casual view. "I'm sorry, I didn't mean to—"

"Some things aren't for your writer's curiosity." His jaw works beneath his beard, hands clenched at his sides. "Some things are off-limits."

"Emma?" The name slips out, remembered from whispers in the diner.

Jackson goes absolutely still, a predator caught in unexpected territory. "You know nothing about her."

"I know she was your fiancée. That she died in a climbing accident." The words tumble out despite the warning signs, my journalist's instinct overriding common sense. "I know that's why you're so—"

"So what?" He steps closer, looming over me, his voice dropping to a dangerous quiet. "Cautious? Insistent that unprepared tourists stay off my mountain? Unwilling to let another person die because they underestimated nature?"

Heat rises in my cheeks. "You're arrogant. Acting like you own the mountain, deciding who's worthy to climb it."

"Arrogant?" A harsh laugh escapes him. "You ignored every warning, risked your life and mine, and you call me arrogant?"

"Yes, arrogant." Standing my ground despite the throb in my ankle. "You took one look at me and decided I was some helpless city girl who couldn't possibly understand your precious wilderness."

"And was I wrong?" He gestures broadly at our situation, voice rising. "Look where we are. Look what happened."

"That doesn't give you the right to dictate what others can do."

"When their stupidity endangers lives? Yes, it absolutely does."

We're inches apart now, both breathing hard, neither willing to back down. His eyes blaze with controlled fury, his scent—pine and smoke and something distinctly male—surrounds me.

"My 'stupidity' is the reason I have a career at all." The words burst out, raw and honest. "Playing it safe my entire life got me nowhere. Taking risks is how I finally broke through."

"There's a difference between calculated risks and reckless endangerment," Jackson growls. "You didn't respect the mountain. You didn't respect the storm. You didn't respect *my* warning."

"I didn't respect your authority, you mean." My chin lifts defiantly. "Because despite what everyone in that town seems to think, you're not actually in charge of—"

His mouth crashes against mine, cutting off the words. The kiss is nothing like I imagined—not that I've imagined kissing this infuriating man—but it's fierce, desperate, and consuming. His hands frame my face, rough calluses against my skin, holding me as if I might disappear.

For one suspended moment, shock prevents any response. Then something primal takes over, and I'm kissing him back with equal fervor, fingers gripping the front of his shirt. The heat between us has nothing to do with the wood-stove and everything to do with days of tension finally igniting.

Days?

Okay, ONE day, but that tension...

His tongue sweeps against mine, demanding and skilled, drawing an embarrassing sound from deep in my throat. Jackson's body presses closer, solid, warm, and overwhelming.

Then, as suddenly as it began, it ends. Jackson wrenches himself away, stumbling backward, eyes wide with what can only be described as horror.

"Fuck." The word explodes from him, rough and raw. "I shouldn't have—"

My lips still tingle, my body humming with unexpected desire. Words fail me completely.

Jackson runs a hand through his hair, agitation in every movement. "This is exactly why—" He stops, jaw working. "I can't do this."

"Jackson—"

"Don't." He holds up a hand, avoiding my gaze. "That was a mistake. A serious lapse in judgment."

The dismissal stings more than it should. "That's one way to describe it."

His eyes finally meet mine, conflicted and stormy. "I can't trust myself around you."

Before I can respond, he grabs his heavy coat from its hook, shoving his arms into sleeves with jerky movements.

"What are you doing?" Alarm cuts through my confusion. "You can't go out there."

"I need air." He yanks a wool hat over his dark hair and reaches for gloves.

"It's a blizzard!" My voice rises with genuine fear. "You just finished lecturing me about mountain safety."

"I know this mountain better than I know myself." He checks a compass and tucks it into his pocket. "I'll follow the guide rope to the storage cache and back. Half hour, max."

"That's insane." I step toward him, forgetting my injured ankle, and stumble.

Jackson instinctively reaches out to steady me, then pulls back as if burned by the contact. "I'll be fine."

"You can't leave." The words come out more pleading than I intend. "It's not safe."

"Neither is staying right here." His expression shutters, all emotion locked away. "The radio's on the table. Crank it every hour to check in with base. If I'm not back in three hours—" He hesitates. "Tell them where I went."

The door opens, admitting a violent blast of snow and wind before slamming shut behind him, leaving me alone in the sudden silence.

"Dammit!" My palm slams against the wooden wall in frustration.

What just happened? One moment, we're arguing; the next, we're kissing as if our lives depend on it, and then he's storming out into a deadly blizzard rather than spend another minute in my presence.

I hobble to the window, pressing my face against the cold glass. Nothing is visible but swirling white. The storm has already swallowed Jackson. Worry gnaws at my insides, along with a healthy dose of anger. How dare he risk his life to avoid dealing with an awkward situation? How dare he kiss me like that, and then flee as if I'm the one who initiated it?

More importantly, how dare my body still hum with awareness, still crave his touch?

The shelter feels cavernous without his commanding presence, the silence oppressive. I busy myself with tasks—stoking the fire, organizing supplies, anything to avoid dwelling on the pressure of his lips against mine, the strength in his hands, the solid warmth of his body.

Minutes stretch into an hour. I crank the radio as instructed, reporting that all remains well at the shelter, carefully omitting that Jackson has ventured out. No need to worry others yet. He said he'd be back.

The second hour passes more slowly, worry crystallizing into genuine fear. The storm shows no signs of abating, if anything intensifying.

What if he lost the guide rope? What if he slipped? What if he's lying injured somewhere on the mountain, slowly freezing while I sit helplessly in this shelter?

By the third hour, I've prepared myself to radio for help, rehearsing how to explain that the mountain's most experienced guide has vanished into a blizzard rather than deal with an unwanted attraction.

The door suddenly bangs open, admitting a snow-covered figure. Jackson staggers inside, ice crusting his beard and eyebrows, his skin frightening pale where visible.

Relief floods me so powerfully that my knees nearly buckle. "You're alive."

He secures the door against the howling wind before turning to face me. His eyes look hollow, exhausted, but his expression reveals nothing of what he's been thinking during his dangerous excursion.

"Told you I would be." His voice sounds rough, as if unused for days rather than hours.

"You're half-frozen."

"I'm fine." He shrugs off his ice-encrusted coat, hanging it mechanically by the door.

"Three hours in a blizzard isn't 'fine,' Jackson." Anger resurfaces now that fear has subsided. "That was reckless."

A bitter smile twists his mouth. "Perhaps you're rubbing off on me."

He moves to the woodstove, holding his hands toward the heat, back deliberately turned to me.

Clear message: conversation over.

The silence stretches between us, taut and uncomfortable. The kiss hovers in the air like an unexploded bomb, neither of us willing to acknowledge it.

Jackson remains by the fire, his shoulders rigid with tension, while I stand awkwardly beside the table, uncertain whether to push or retreat.

"I won't ask where you went." The words emerge softer than intended.

"Good." He doesn't turn around.

"But I will ask why."

His back stiffens further. "You know why."

"Because you kissed me?"

"Because I lost control." He finally turns, eyes guarded. "I don't lose control. Ever."

The implications hang heavy between us. Lost control with me. Lost control on the mountain once before, with tragic consequences.

"It was just a kiss." The lie tastes bitter on my tongue. It wasn't *just* anything, and we both know it.

"Nothing is *'just'* anything up here." He gestures toward the raging storm outside. "Everything has consequences. Everything."

His intensity should repel me. Instead, it draws me like a magnet. This man feels everything so deeply and guards himself so carefully that the momentary lapse in his armor reveals depths I hadn't imagined.

"We're stuck here regardless." I attempt practicality. "We can't exactly avoid each other."

"We can avoid talking about it." His tone suggests the matter is closed. "And it won't happen again."

The finality in his voice stings more than it should. Not that I want it to happen again. Absolutely not. This man is infuriating, arrogant, damaged, and completely wrong for me in every conceivable way.

So why does my body tingle at the memory of his touch?

Why does disappointment curl through me at his dismissal?

Jackson moves to the generator, checking it, deliberately focusing elsewhere. The message is clear: boundaries are re-established, walls are rebuilt, and they are stronger than before.

But beneath his controlled exterior, tension radiates from him like heat. And despite his declaration, something elemental shifted between us—something neither of us can pretend away.

The blizzard rages outside, trapping us together for days to come. The kiss may not happen again, but its aftershocks will continue reverberating through our forced proximity, making the wilderness outside seem far less dangerous than the smoldering tension within these four walls.

Angel's Peak

CHAPTER 4

POWER FAILURE

DAWN CREEPS THROUGH THE FROSTED WINDOW, casting weak gray light across the shelter's interior. Another day trapped on this mountain, another day confined with Jackson Hart.

Sleep came in restless bursts, and whenever I closed my eyes, my mind replayed yesterday's kiss. The pressure of his mouth, the strength in his hands, the unexpectedness of it all—these sensations haunted the thin line between wakefulness and dreams.

Jackson sits at the small table, working on the generator again. Judging by the fresh coffee and rekindled fire, he's been up for hours. His movements are precise and focused as if the machine before him holds all the answers to the universe. He hasn't acknowledged my waking, though the creaking of the cot surely gave me away.

"Morning." My voice sounds unnaturally loud in the quiet shelter.

Jackson's shoulders tense slightly, the only indication he's heard me. His attention remains fixed on the generator's innards, the screwdriver twisting harder than it seems like it should.

Two can play at this game. I swing my legs over the edge of the cot, testing my ankle. The throbbing has subsided to a dull ache—painful but manageable. Using the makeshift cane, I make my way to the woodstove, where a pot of water sits warming.

The routine of morning ablutions provides welcome distraction. The cold water against my face stings pleasantly, washing away the lingering cobwebs of sleep. My reflection in the small mirror hung by the door reveals tangled hair and shadows beneath my eyes. Not my best look, but vanity seems ridiculous under the circumstances.

"Coffee's hot." Jackson's voice, when it finally comes, is neutral, professional—as if yesterday never happened.

"Thanks." I pour the dark liquid into a metal mug, the rich aroma momentarily overwhelming the shelter's persistent scents of wood smoke and close quarters.

The generator suddenly sputters, lights flickering before stabilizing. Jackson mutters something under his breath, adjusting a component with quick, sure fingers.

"Problem?" I venture, sipping the strong coffee.

"Fuel line's clogged. Been fighting it all morning." He doesn't look up. "Running on borrowed time."

"Meaning?"

"Meaning when it dies, it dies." Now he glances up, those piercing blue eyes meeting mine briefly before returning to his work. "We lose power. No lights, no radio, no heat except the woodstove."

The implications settle heavily. "How long do we have?"

"Hours, maybe. Not days." He tightens a connection with grim determination. "Need to prepare while we can."

Jackson outlines our contingency plan. We're to melt extra snow for water while we still have the electric kettle. Move essential supplies closer to the woodstove. Inventory the lantern fuel. Check our wood supply.

We fall into an uneasy rhythm, working around each other in the small space, carefully maintaining distance while completing necessary tasks. The deliberate avoidance of yesterday's events hangs between us, an invisible barrier more solid than the shelter's stone walls.

The generator coughs again, lights dimming momentarily.

"Not good." Jackson straightens from his crouch beside it. "We need to conserve what power remains. Essential functions only."

"What's essential?" My notebook lies on the table, beckoning. Perhaps this forced working relationship provides the perfect opportunity for my article—professional distance as a shield against whatever sparked between us yesterday.

"Heat. Communication. Light, but only when absolutely necessary." He moves to the radio, cranking it with practiced turns of his wrist.

"Angel's Peak Base, this is Hart. Radio check, over." His voice takes on a formal quality when speaking into the device.

Static crackles before a response comes through. "Copy, Hart. Reading you five-by-five. Status update?"

"Generator failing. Will maintain scheduled check-ins as long as possible. Storm status?"

"No improvement. System stalled over the range. Expect another forty-eight hours minimum. How are your supplies?"

"Adequate. Will update at next check-in. Hart out." He sets the radio aside, expression grim.

Two more days, at least. The knowledge should dismay me, but beneath the practical concerns lies an unexpected flutter of something else. Two more days with this complex, frustrating man who kisses like he's drowning and I'm air.

Ridiculous thoughts. Focus on the article.

I retrieve my notebook and pen, settling at the table while Jackson checks our wood supply.

"Mind if I ask you some questions? For my article?" The professional tone comes naturally, with years of interviews lending confidence to my voice.

Jackson pauses, arms full of split logs. "Your article."

"Yes, the reason I came to Angel's Peak in the first place. 'Hidden Treasures of the Rockies,' remember?"

A muscle ticks in his jaw. "Hard to forget, considering where we are."

"I'm not asking about—" My hand gestures vaguely toward the shelf where Emma's photo sits. "Just about the mountains. Your expertise. What draws people here."

He deposits the logs beside the woodstove, stacking them neatly. Several moments pass before he speaks, as if weighing the pros and cons of cooperation.

"Ask your questions." The words come reluctantly, a concession rather than enthusiasm.

I flip to a fresh page, pen poised. "How long have you been guiding in these mountains?"

"Fifteen years professionally. Whole life unofficially." He remains standing, arms crossed over his broad chest. "Grandfather taught me to climb when I was six."

"What makes Angel's Peak special compared to other locations in the Rockies?"

Something shifts in his expression—a softening around the eyes, a subtle relaxation of his perpetual frown. "Diversity. Within twenty square miles, you get alpine meadows, technical rock faces, old-growth forest, three lakes, vineyards, and summits that challenge even veteran climbers."

"Vineyards? In Colorado?"

"Yeah, surprised me too, but it's a surprisingly lucrative cottage industry."

"What else can you tell me?"

His voice warms as he continues, describing hidden waterfalls accessible only by unmarked trails, rare flowers that bloom for just two weeks each summer, and rock formations sculpted by millennia of wind and weather. Passion threads through his words, transforming the taciturn mountain man into an eloquent advocate for this wilderness he clearly loves.

I scribble notes rapidly, captivated by this glimpse behind his guarded exterior. "What's your favorite season here?"

"Fall." The answer comes without hesitation. "September, specifically. Summer crowds gone, winter tourists not yet arrived. The aspens turn gold, days clear and cool, nights crisp enough for campfires. Perfect climbing weather."

My pen stills as I picture it—Jackson in his element, scaling rock faces painted with autumn colors, utterly at peace. The image tugs at something unexpected within me.

"And for someone like me—a beginner—what would you recommend? If we weren't, you know, trapped in a blizzard." A small attempt at humor to lighten the intensity.

His eyes narrow slightly. "Someone like you."

"A city girl with limited outdoor experience but willing to learn." The qualifier tumbles out, surprising me with its sincerity.

Jackson studies me for a long moment as if seeing me anew. "Ridge Trail to Mirror Lake. Four miles round trip, moderate difficulty. Best at sunrise when the mountains reflect perfectly in the water. Worth every step."

The generator sputters violently, drawing his attention. He kneels beside it, adjustments increasingly futile as it coughs and protests.

"Would you take me there?" The question escapes before prudence can contain it. "When this is over, I mean. For the article."

His hands still on the machine. "You'd trust me to guide you after this?"

"You're the best, according to everyone in town, and you did save me. That makes you the best guide within fifteen feet." My attempt at humor falls flat. "Despite our... differences, I'd be foolish to choose anyone else."

Something unreadable flickers across his features. Before he can respond, the generator emits a high-pitched whine followed by alarming silence.

The lights flicker once, twice, then die completely.

"That's it." Jackson's voice comes through the sudden dimness. "We're officially on survival mode."

Outside, the blizzard howls with renewed vengeance, wind battering the shelter's walls. Without the generator's steady hum, every creak and groan of the structure amplifies, the storm's fury no longer background noise but immediate presence.

The temperature drops perceptibly within minutes, the woodstove's heat insufficient to counter the biting cold seeping through every crack. Jackson moves, stoking the fire higher, positioning reflective surfaces to maximize warmth.

"Move closer to the stove." His silhouette looms larger in the firelight. "Body heat's precious now."

I relocate to the floor near the woodstove; my notebook clutched like a shield. Jackson settles nearby, close enough for safety but maintaining a careful distance. The firelight catches the planes of his face, highlighting cheekbones and casting shadows beneath his brow. Unfairly handsome, even—especially—in this primal setting.

Hours pass in strained silence, broken only by necessary communication. The cold intensifies despite the fire's best efforts. My fingers grow stiff around my pen, and my notes become increasingly illegible.

"You're shivering." Jackson observes, watching me attempt to suppress another violent tremor.

"I'm fine." The chattering of my teeth betrays the lie.

"You're hypothermic." He rises, retrieving a heavy woolen blanket from the cot. Instead of simply handing it to me, he settles beside me, draping the blanket over our shoulders.

The sudden proximity steals my breath. His body radiates heat, solid and substantial against my side. Every nerve ending springs to alert awareness, hyper-focused on each point of contact—shoulder to shoulder, hip to hip, thigh to thigh.

"Conservation of resources." His voice rumbles close to my ear, sending entirely different shivers down my spine. "Basic survival."

"Right. Survival." The word emerges breathier than intended.

Beneath the blanket, warmth blooms between us, chasing away the numbing cold. His scent surrounds me—pine and wood smoke and something uniquely him, masculine and oddly comforting.

"Better?" The question carries unexpected gentleness.

"Yes." Truth, though not entirely because of the physical warmth.

Firelight dances across the shelter's interior, casting everything in amber and shadow. Time loses meaning, measured now by the gradual return of sensation to my fingertips, the rhythmic rise and fall of Jackson's chest beside mine, and the occasional crack of burning wood.

"Tell me about your writing." His request breaks the silence, surprising me.

"What do you want to know?"

"Why this article matters so much. Worth risking everything for."

The question deserves honesty. "It's my chance. Three years writing fluff pieces about tourist traps and overpriced restaurants, following someone else's formula. This is the first assignment where they're letting me choose the angle and find the story beneath the surface."

"And what story are you finding?" His gaze remains on the fire, profile strong in the flickering light.

"I thought it was about hidden natural wonders." My voice softens. "Now I'm not so sure."

"What changed?"

My turn to watch the flames. "Met a mountain guide who sees these peaks as more than scenery or adventure. Someone who respects their power and understands their dangers. Makes for a more complex narrative."

His shoulders tense slightly beneath the blanket. "Don't make me your story, Cloe."

My name on his lips sends an unexpected thrill through me. It's the first time he's used it directly.

"Everyone has a story." The firelight emboldens me. "Yours is compelling."

"Mine is private." The words lack their usual edge, softened by our shared warmth.

"Fair enough." I concede, shifting slightly to ease my position. The movement brings us closer, my head now resting naturally against his shoulder. Neither of us acknowledges this new proximity, though the tension in his body suggests acute awareness.

"What about your story?" he asks after several heartbeats of silence. "The one that doesn't make it into the magazine article."

The question catches me off-guard. "Nothing exciting. I had a middle-class upbringing in Burlington, overprotective parents, college, a journalism degree, and an endless string of entry-level positions."

"And here you are, defying death on a mountain." Something like understanding colors his tone. "Proving them wrong."

The insight strikes uncomfortably close to the truth. "Maybe."

"Some things aren't worth proving, Cloe." His voice drops lower, intimate in the diminishing firelight. "Some risks aren't worth taking."

"Says the man who climbs mountains for a living." My attempt at lightness fails, words emerging with unexpected vulnerability.

"I respect the risks. Account for them. Prepare." His head turns toward mine, his breath warm against my temple. "There's a difference between courage and recklessness."

Our faces are inches apart now, his eyes reflecting golden firelight. The blanket creates a cocoon around us, sealing us in shared warmth and suddenly electric tension.

"And which am I?" The question barely makes it past my lips.

"I haven't decided yet." His gaze drops to my mouth, lingering with unmistakable intent.

My heart thunders against my ribs. The attraction between us pulses like a living entity in the darkened shelter. His face inches closer, almost imperceptibly, the magnetism drawing us together despite every logical objection.

Our lips hover a breath apart, the promise of connection humming in the diminishing space between us.

The woodstove suddenly cracks violently—a log splitting from internal pressure. The sound shatters the moment, and Jackson pulls back as if burned, the spell broken.

He clears his throat, adjusting the blanket around us but maintaining the new distance. "We should conserve energy. Try to sleep."

Disappointment floods me, irrational and powerful. "Right."

"I'll keep the fire going." He makes no move to leave our shared blanket, the practical necessity of warmth outweighing whatever boundaries he's trying to maintain.

The storm continues its assault outside, wind screaming

around the shelter's corners. Inside, different forces rage—attraction, resistance, the undeniable pull between two people fighting it for entirely different reasons.

In the deepening darkness, with only firelight to see by, Jackson's presence beside me becomes my entire world—his steady breathing, solid warmth, and the careful distance he maintains even while physics and survival demand our closeness.

The night stretches before us, long and cold, with nothing but this blanket and each other standing between us and the killing cold. And in the flickering shadows, one truth becomes increasingly clear: the power failure outside is nothing compared to the one happening within—the steady collapse of the barriers we've built to keep each other at a safe distance.

Angel's Peak

Chapter 5

Cold Truths

Morning arrives with cruel clarity. Three days trapped on this mountain, and the temperature inside the shelter has plummeted to a point where my breath forms visible clouds with each exhale. The generator's absence has transformed our shelter from merely rustic to brutally primitive.

Jackson kneels by the woodstove, coaxing flames from fresh kindling. His movements are practiced and efficient, shoulders hunched against the cold. Frost glitters in his dark beard, evidence of his pre-dawn excursion to retrieve more firewood from the outdoor cache.

"Storm's weakening." He doesn't look up from his task. "Another day, maybe two."

Hope flutters briefly before reality dampens it. Even when the blizzard stops, the mountain will remain treacherous—deep snow, hidden crevasses, avalanche risks. Our imprisonment simply shifts from weather-enforced to safety-mandated.

My ankle throbs less today, healing despite the circumstances. Small mercies.

"Water's low." Jackson gestures toward our dwindling supply. "Need to melt snow."

This has become our morning routine—assessing resources, planning for survival, speaking in truncated sentences as if full thoughts might consume too much precious energy. The cold has a way of stripping communication to essentials.

Jackson hands me a small pot. "Fresh snow from the lee side. Less contaminated."

Stepping outside requires wrapping myself in every available layer—my coat plus an extra woolen shirt from Jackson's supplies. The cold still slices through, stealing breath and sensation within seconds.

The snow is deep and pristine, piling against the shelter's eastern wall. I fill the pot quickly, my fingers already numbing despite my thick gloves. The landscape stretches white in every direction, with mountains barely distinguishable from the sky in the uniform grayness.

Back inside, the shelter's relative warmth feels like a furnace by comparison. Jackson takes the snow-filled pot, placing it on the woodstove's surface.

"Always melt snow before drinking, " he demonstrates, stirring the gradually liquefying contents. "Eating it directly lowers your core temperature. It can kill you faster than dehydration."

The morning unfolds in similar lessons—practical knowledge disguised as instructions. How to maximize caloric intake from limited food. How to layer clothing for optimal insulation. How to recognize early signs of frostbite.

Jackson proves a surprisingly patient teacher. His usual gruffness softens when sharing wilderness wisdom and is replaced by focused intensity. When I master a knot he's shown me—useful for securing gear in high winds—something like approval flickers across his features.

"Quick learner." The words emerge reluctantly, as if praising me costs him something.

"Good teacher." The exchange feels significant, a small bridge spanning the chasm between us.

By midday, our activities have warmed the shelter marginally. Jackson rations two protein bars between us for lunch—sustenance without satisfaction. My stomach grumbles in protest, accustomed to more substantial fare.

"Gets easier." Jackson notices my expression as I chew the bland, dense rectangle. "Hunger. Body adjusts."

"Speaking from experience?"

He nods once. "Ten days stranded on McKinley. Rescue delayed by weather. Similar to this."

"Ten days?" The prospect of seven more days like these three sends panic skittering through me.

"Different circumstances. Worse injuries. Less shelter." His gaze travels to the window, where snow continues to fall steadily, if less violently than before. "We're fortunate by comparison."

Fortunate. Not a word I'd have chosen for our situation, yet his perspective shifts mine slightly. We have shelter. Heat. Food. Each other. The last thought lingers uncomfortably.

The afternoon stretches endlessly before us. Without power for light, the shelter dims as clouds thicken outside. Jackson lights our precious lantern, conserving fuel by keeping the flame low. The resulting shadows dance across the stone walls, creating an almost intimate atmosphere despite the cold.

"We need distraction." Jackson retrieves a battered deck of cards from a shelf. "Mental activity helps combat cold."

He deals a hand of gin rummy, explaining rules I already know, but allow him to review. The normalcy of the activity strikes me as bizarrely comforting—two people playing cards while a blizzard rages outside, as if this were some planned vacation rather than a survival scenario.

Three hands in, the game has generated more conversation than the previous days combined. Jackson reveals small details about himself—preferred climbing routes, a surprising fondness for classical music, and his grandfather's role in establishing Angel's Peak's first rescue team.

My journalistic instincts prickle with interest, but I resist the urge to interrogate. This fragile camaraderie feels too valuable to risk.

During the fourth hand, my gaze drifts to the shelf where Emma's photograph sits partially hidden. In the lantern's soft glow, the frame catches light, drawing attention like a beacon.

Jackson follows my glance, his expression shuttering immediately. The comfortable atmosphere dissipates like smoke.

"Your fiancée was beautiful." The words emerge before wisdom can contain them.

His hands still on the cards, knuckles whitening. For several heartbeats, I'm certain he'll retreat behind anger again, ending our tentative connection.

Instead, he carefully places his cards face down.

"Yes." The single syllable carries volumes of pain.

Silence stretches between us, taut with unspoken grief. I've crossed a boundary, yet something tells me it needed crossing.

"Would you tell me about her?" My voice softens, setting aside the journalist for simple human connection. "Not for the article. Just... because."

Jackson's jaw works beneath his beard. His eyes remain fixed on the tabletop, seeing something far beyond the weathered wood.

"Emma Mitchell. Twenty-nine when she died. Environmental scientist. Specialized in alpine ecosystems." The words emerge stilted at first, facts without emotion, as if reading a biography. "Expert climber. Better than me on technical ascents. Fearless. Brilliant."

He rises abruptly, moving to retrieve the photograph. His fingers trace the frame with reverence before he returns to the table.

"Three years ago. Leading a group of university researchers up the north face. Routine climb—challenging but within their abilities." His voice changes, roughening. "Storm warning came through late. Too late. Should have turned back immediately."

The photograph trembles slightly in his grip.

"Emma wanted to push forward. Just another hour, she said. They needed specific samples from the summit. Important research." His eyes finally meet mine, haunted. "I agreed. Against my better judgment. Against everything I knew about the mountain."

The confession hangs between us, heavy with self-recrimination.

"The storm hit faster than anyone predicted. Visibility dropped to nothing. Temperatures plummeted." His thumb brushes Emma's smiling face. "We were making our descent. She was leading the second group."

My heart constricts, already knowing where this story ends but dreading the details.

"Avalanche." The word emerges like broken glass. "Small one. Just enough. She was swept over a ledge. Rope snapped." His breathing becomes uneven. "I couldn't reach her in time. Couldn't... couldn't save her."

Grief radiates from him in palpable waves. Without thinking, I reach across the table, covering his hand with mine.

"It wasn't your fault."

His laugh emerges bitter, hollow. "Everyone says that. But I made the call. I was responsible. Her blood is on my hands."

"You couldn't have known—"

"I *should* have known." His voice rises slightly, raw with

emotion. "That's literally my job. Reading the mountain. Predicting the unpredictable. Keeping people safe. Her blood is on my hands."

The words hit like a punch to the gut—not just for what they reveal, but for everything they explain.

Suddenly, it all makes sense. The fury in his voice when he found me on that ledge, the way he barked commands without mercy, dragging me up the mountain like I was an unruly rookie, his coldness, his distance, his refusal to look at me like a person and only as a liability.

It wasn't about me.

It was about her.

Emma.

And I see it now—the way grief and guilt have carved themselves into his bones. The weight he's carried, blaming himself for a choice made in a moment, for something that might never have been avoidable no matter what he did.

My heart aches not for Emma, but for him. For the silent suffering I hadn't seen before. I was too caught up in my own pride and frustration to notice the cracks beneath his armor.

It wasn't about Jackson hating city people or assuming I was fragile and helpless.

It was about loss.

Or fear.

It was about watching someone fall and knowing—knowing—he couldn't bring them back.

And me?

I was another Emma in the making.

I swallow hard, my voice soft. "That's why you were so angry with me."

His eyes flash to mine, sharp and surprised.

"You saw me up there and thought—" My throat tightens. "You thought it was happening again."

His jaw works, but he says nothing.

"You didn't hate me," I whisper. "You were terrified."

He doesn't nod. Doesn't confirm it aloud.

He doesn't have to.

I see it now. Not a cold, infuriating mountain man—but a protector. One who's already lost too much and will burn the world down before he lets it happen again.

For the first time since we met, I don't feel dismissed or underestimated.

I feel seen.

And safe.

"You can't blame yourself." An unexpected anger flares in me. "One terrible accident doesn't erase all the lives you've saved. All the people you've guided safely? All the rescues you've performed?"

His eyes narrow. "You don't understand—"

"I understand guilt. I understand grief. But I also understand Emma chose to be on that mountain. She was an expert climber who made her own decisions."

"It's not that simple."

"No, it's not. Nothing about loss is simple." My voice softens. "But punishing yourself forever won't bring her back. And it won't honor what she loved about the mountains, climbing, taking necessary risks for things that matter."

Jackson withdraws his hand from mine, but instead of retreating into coldness, he simply looks... tired. Bone-deep exhausted from carrying his guilt for so long.

"Why do you care?" The question contains genuine bewilderment. "You barely know me."

The answer requires honesty I'm not sure I'm ready to give. "Because I recognize someone running from themselves. I've been doing it my whole life."

His eyebrows lift slightly, inviting elaboration.

"My parents..." I pause, organizing thoughts rarely verbalized. "They meant well, but from the moment I was diagnosed with childhood leukemia, they treated me like I was made of glass. No sports. Limited outdoor activities. Constant monitoring. Every cough was a crisis."

"You had cancer?"

"Had and beat. It's been over twenty years. I was little, a toddler. My memories of what happened are fuzzy."

"Is that why they were overprotective?"

"I suppose. I beat the cancer, but they were always looking for the other shoe to drop. I could barely breathe." The memories surface with surprising clarity—the sidelines I was relegated to, the adventures forbidden, the pitying glances from classmates.

"They convinced everyone, including me, that I was fragile." My fingers trace patterns on the rough tabletop. "College was my escape. But even then, their voices stayed in my head. 'Be careful, Cloe. Don't push yourself, Cloe. Know your limitations, Cloe.'"

Jackson listens with unexpected intensity, his focus complete.

"Journalism became my rebellion. Particularly travel writing." A small smile tugs at my lips. "Every assignment was proof that their expectations didn't bind me. Every risk I took was a middle finger to years of cautionary tales."

Understanding dawns in his eyes. "Including hiking alone in a blizzard."

"Including that." Shame colors my admission. "In my defense, it wasn't a blizzard when I started out."

"You *were* warned."

"Not my proudest moment."

"We all have those." His voice holds no judgment now.

Silence settles between us, not uncomfortable but contemplative. Outside, the wind has calmed to a steady moan rather than its previous howl. The lantern flickers, shadows shifting across Jackson's features, softening his customary intensity.

"So we're both running." His observation comes quietly. "Me from guilt, you from being underestimated."

"Pretty much."

"And now we're stuck here. Nowhere to run."

The irony makes me laugh out loud, surprising us both with its warmth. "The Universe has a twisted sense of humor."

A hint of a smile tugs at Jackson's mouth—the first I've seen. The expression transforms him, cracking the stoic facade to reveal something warmer beneath.

"Emma would have appreciated the cosmic joke." His tone carries fondness among the grief. "She always said mountains had their own wisdom."

"She sounds remarkable."

"She was." His fingers trace her photograph once more before carefully returning it to the shelf. This time, he leaves it visible rather than hidden. A small but significant change.

Night approaches rapidly, darkness gathering in the shelter's corners despite the lantern's valiant efforts. The temperature drops further as the sun abandons us, cold seeping through walls designed to withstand wind but not to retain heat.

"We should conserve the lantern fuel." Jackson eyes the flame critically.

Darkness falls completely when he extinguishes the light, leaving only the woodstove's orange glow. Our world narrows to this small circle of warmth, the boundaries of the shelter fading into shadow.

"Come closer to the fire." Jackson's voice emerges from the dimness. "Body heat is critical tonight."

We arrange blankets on the floor near the stove, necessity overriding awkwardness. The shared vulnerability of our earlier conversations lingers, creating a different atmosphere than previous nights.

Jackson settles beside me, close enough that our shoulders touch. The contact sends awareness skittering across my skin despite the layers between us.

"Thank you." His words emerge so quietly I almost miss them. "For listening. About Emma."

"Thank you for telling me."

Minutes pass in companionable silence, broken only by the fire's occasional pop and crackle. The darkness creates a strange intimacy, as if we exist in a world unto ourselves, separated from reality.

"I've never told anyone the full story." His confession emerges quietly. "Not even the investigation team."

The trust implied in this admission sends warmth through me, unrelated to the fire's heat.

"Why me?" The question emerges unbidden.

Jackson shifts slightly, his profile illuminated by flames. "Because you push. Because you don't accept the surface answer. Because..."

He pauses, struggling visibly with words.

"Because I shouldn't want to tell you anything, but I do." The confession emerges rough-edged, reluctant. "I shouldn't notice how your eyes change color in different light. Shouldn't care about your childhood or your parents or your career ambitions. Shouldn't think about your mouth when I'm collecting firewood."

My breath catches, and my heart accelerates wildly.

"But I do." His voice drops lower, rumbling through the darkness. "God help me, I do."

The confession hovers between us, impossible to ignore or dismiss. Heat that has nothing to do with the woodstove floods through me.

"If we're being honest, I shouldn't wonder what would

have happened if the generator hadn't broken last night." My admission emerges slightly breathless. "I shouldn't replay that kiss every time I close my eyes. I shouldn't imagine your hands on me instead of just your shoulder against mine."

Jackson's breath audibly catches. "Cloe—"

"But I do." The truth flows easier in darkness. "I know it's inconvenient and complicated and probably temporary. But whatever it is—it feels more real than anything I've known."

His hand finds mine in the shadows, fingers intertwining with deliberate intent. The simple contact sends electricity racing up my arm.

"This is a terrible idea." His voice has roughened, deeper than before.

"Absolutely terrible."

"You're leaving in days. Back to your life."

"And you're staying here. Back to yours."

Our hands remain connected despite these practical objections, neither willing to break the tentative contact.

"So what do we do?" The question hangs between us, loaded with possibilities.

The fire casts flickering shadows across his features, highlighting the warring emotions there—desire, hesitation, need, restraint. His thumb traces circles on my palm, each movement sending shivers through me.

"I don't know." Honesty colors his response. "But pretending this isn't happening isn't working anymore."

The admission cracks something open between us—the final barrier of denial. Attraction crackles in the small space separating our bodies, palpable as the cold pressing against the shelter's walls.

"No," I agree softly. "It's not."

Our gazes lock in the firelight, unspoken desire reflected between us. The decision point looms, heavy with potential consequences—for hearts, for boundaries, for the careful distance we've maintained despite close physical proximity.

Whatever path we choose, one truth emerges: the real storm was never the blizzard raging outside but the emotions brewing between two people who found each other at exactly the wrong time, in exactly the wrong place.

Angel's Peak

Chapter 6

Burning Up

Morning arrives differently this time. No stark boundary between night and awakening, but a gradual awareness of warmth, of Jackson's steady breathing beside me, of our hands still intertwined despite hours of sleep.

Everything has changed.

The admission of attraction hangs in the air between us, transforming the atmosphere inside our small shelter. Each glance carries new weight. Each casual touch sparks awareness that neither of us can pretend to ignore any longer.

Jackson rises first, stoking the dying embers in the wood stove. Muscles shift beneath his thermal shirt as he works. His movements are economical and precise. My eyes track him with newfound freedom, no longer hiding my appreciation behind journalistic interest.

He turns, catching my gaze. Something flares in his eyes—heat, hunger, a flash of uncertainty.

"Sleep okay?" His voice carries morning roughness that sends a shiver down my spine.

"Better than expected." The floor beside the stove should have been uncomfortable, yet nestled against his solid warmth,

I slept more soundly than any night since our confinement began.

Jackson measures coffee grounds into the pot, his movements deliberate, almost hesitant. The easy connection of last night's conversation has given way to something more charged, crackling with potential energy.

"About last night..." He sets the pot on the stove, back still turned to me.

"We don't have to talk about it." My pulse quickens, unsure whether he regrets our admissions.

"We do." Now he faces me, expression guarded yet determined. "I need to be clear about something."

"Okay." The warmth in my chest cools slightly, preparing for rejection.

"I don't do relationships." His jaw sets firmly, eyes locked on mine. "Haven't since Emma. Don't plan to start now."

The declaration should sting, yet something in his stance —the tension in his shoulders, the careful control in his voice —suggests this costs him. The words aren't as simple as they sound.

"I'm not asking for one." Rising from my blanket nest, I meet his gaze evenly. "After this, I'll be back in Burlington finishing my article, and you'll be here, doing whatever mountain men do when they're not rescuing foolish writers."

"Mountain men?" His eyebrow lifts slightly.

"You know what I mean." A small smile tugs at my lips despite the seriousness of the conversation. "What happens in this shelter can stay in this shelter. No expectations, no complications."

"You say that now." Jackson studies me, searching for something in my expression.

"Because I mean it." Closing the distance between us, I stop just short of touching him. "I'm not looking to be your redemption story, Jackson. Or your second chance. Or your great love. I'm just..."

"Just what?" His voice drops lower, intimate in the small space between us.

"Just drawn to you. Against all logic and reason."

His breath audibly catches. The coffee pot begins to bubble, forgotten.

Heat coils in the narrow space between us, thick and charged, sparking against my skin like static before a storm. His chest rises and falls in measured rhythm, but his eyes—glacier blue and darkened with something far more dangerous than cold—are locked on mine like a man fighting gravity and losing.

His hand brushes my arm, fingertips grazing the sensitive skin just inside my elbow, and the contact ignites a trail of fire straight to my core. I feel it everywhere—low in my belly, in the pulse behind my knees, and in the ache that blooms with every second of silence stretched tight between us.

"You're shivering," he murmurs, voice rough, but it's not the cold we're talking about anymore.

"I'm not cold," I breathe.

A muscle ticks in his jaw. His hand lifts higher, cupping the side of my neck, thumb stroking the hollow just beneath my jaw—delicate, reverent, like he's memorizing the shape of me.

"I shouldn't," he says, low and ragged. "This is a mistake."

The words lack conviction, undermined by the heat in his gaze. They're already burning up between us, useless against the heat we've stoked.

"Probably."

"I can't offer you anything beyond right now." His thumb stills.

The warning is clear. Stark. He means it—not just a lack

of commitment, but a man already haunted by the past, afraid to offer a future he doesn't believe he deserves.

"I'm not asking for anything beyond right now," I whisper, and I mean it. My body aches for him, for the connection, for the surrender I swore I'd never give again—but tonight, I want it.

I want him.

Something shifts in his expression—restraint gives way to decision. His hand rises, fingers tracing my cheek with unexpected gentleness that contradicts the roughness of his callused skin. His touch is still gentle but no longer hesitant.

"Last chance to back out." His voice rumbles, a warning and invitation combined.

My answer comes in action rather than words, closing the final distance between us, pressing my lips to his—soft at first, but full of heat—and he meets it with fire.

Unlike our first impulsive kiss, this one begins softly, almost tentatively. A question, an exploration. His hands cradle my face as if holding something precious and fragile, belying the strength I know those hands possess.

The gentleness lasts mere moments before hunger takes over. Jackson's arms wrap around me, pulling me against the solid plane of his chest as the kiss deepens. My fingers tangle in his hair, holding him closer, needing more.

Coffee boils over on the stove, sizzling against hot metal. Neither of us moves to save it.

His mouth travels from mine to my jaw and my neck, finding sensitive places I never knew existed. Each press of his lips draws sounds from me that would be embarrassing if I had any capacity for embarrassment left.

"God, you're beautiful." The words brush against my skin, reverent.

My hands explore the contours of his shoulders, the breadth of his back, and the surprising softness of his hair.

Desire builds with each touch, each discovery, pooling low in my abdomen.

"Are you sure about this?" Jackson pulls back slightly, breathing heavily, eyes darkened to midnight blue.

"That depends," I murmur, fingers tracing the rough line of his jaw.

"On what?"

"On whether you're going to just kiss me... or—"

"Or what?" His gaze sharpens, laser-focused.

"Fuck me."

A low growl rumbles from his chest. He steps closer, chest brushing mine, heat radiating off him like fire in the freezing air.

"Oh, I'm definitely going to fuck you." His voice goes from gravel to sin. "Hard. Deep. Until you forget your own goddamn name."

My breath catches.

"I'm going to spread you open on that cot," he continues, his words dark and deliberate, each one striking like a match, "make you beg for it—my fingers, my mouth, my cock—until you can't think straight. And then I'm going to fill you up so good you won't remember why this was a mistake."

Something primal flashes across his features. In one fluid motion, he lifts me, hands gripping my thighs as my legs wrap instinctively around his waist. The raw display of strength sends heat spiraling through me as he carries me the few steps to the narrow cot.

"You're mine. Every inch. Every sound. Every fucking tremble."

He lays me down with surprising care, then stands to remove his thermal shirt. The firelight plays across his torso, illuminating a landscape of muscle and scars—evidence of a life lived in constant negotiation with wilderness and risk.

"What happened?" My eyes widen at a particularly dramatic scar tracking across his left ribs.

There's no way I'm walking out of this unchanged.

"Ice climbing accident. Five years ago." His voice is steady, unbothered, like he's recounting the weather. "Rock broke free, caught me on the way down."

My fingers drift across the scar, the raised line stark against the heat of his skin. "Did it hurt?"

"Not until later." He catches my hand in his and brings it to his mouth. Lips brush my knuckles, a kiss that feels more like a brand. "Adrenaline's one hell of a drug."

The air thickens. Heavy with heat. With want.

He lowers himself onto the cot beside me, our bodies pressed close by necessity and something far more dangerous. His weight, his warmth, the scent of pine and sweat and wood smoke—it coils around me like a drug of its own, making it hard to think.

His hand slips beneath the hem of my thermal top, sliding slowly across bare skin. Warm. Possessive. "May I?"

That simple question—gravel-rough and reverent—sends a bolt of arousal straight through me. The request, so formal amidst such intensity, pulls a smile from me.

"Please."

Clothing disappears in frenzied bursts and fumbling touches. Our movements are hampered by the cot's narrow confines. The cramped space turns every movement into friction, every brush of skin into fire.

Each newly revealed expanse of skin demands exploration —my fingers mapping the contours of his chest, his mouth discovering the sensitive hollow of my collarbone.

He groans when he gets my shirt off, like the sight of my bare chest physically knocks the air from his lungs. His hands span my ribs, thumbs grazing the undersides of my breasts like he's memorizing the way I curve.

Jackson's restraint grows more evident with each passing moment—his breathing harsh, muscles tense beneath my wandering hands, yet his touch remains measured, controlled.

"You don't have to be so careful." My words emerge breathless as his lips trace the curve of my breast. "I won't break."

"Careful was before," he growls. "This? This is what I've been holding back. I've wanted you since I pulled you up that cliff. I've wanted this. Wanted you. Hated myself for it, but fuck, Cloe... I want you so bad I ache."

Something shifts in his expression—a barrier falling, control slipping.

"And you will break," he says. "I can guarantee it."

The confession ignites something primal within me. My nails scrape lightly down his back, drawing a groan that vibrates against my skin.

"Show me."

Angel's Peak

Chapter 7

Until You Break

Jackson's mouth covers my breast, hot and wet and unrelenting. One hand palms the other, thumb flicking over the nipple until I gasp and arch into him. His other hand grips my thigh, spreading me, anchoring me.

Jackson's careful restraint transforms into focused intensity. His hands grip my hips, positioning me beneath him with confident authority. His mouth claims mine in a kiss that borders on possessive, tongue demanding entrance I eagerly grant.

The dominant nature he's kept carefully leashed emerges fully now—in the authoritative press of his body against mine, the controlled strength in his hands as they explore every inch of me, the commanding tone when he murmurs directions against my ear.

"Tell me what you want." His voice drops to a growl that sends shivers racing across my skin.

Words fail me, replaced by inarticulate sounds as his fingers find sensitive places, drawing reactions my body can't disguise.

"Use your words, Cloe." The command comes gently but

firmly. His eyes hold mine, seeking genuine consent amidst the haze of desire.

"You." The word encompasses everything. "All of you. Taking charge. Being...*rough*."

"Music to my ears." His smile tilts, all satisfaction and promise—dark, dangerous promise.

It shouldn't affect me like it does. But the moment those words leave his mouth, heat blooms low in my belly. A slow, molten flood that curls through me, twisting around my spine, stealing my breath.

He notices.

Of course, he notices.

His expression shifts—wolfish, predatory. The kind of look that says he's already undressing my thoughts and peeling back every layer of restraint.

"Interesting." His fingers continue their torturous exploration, skimming over my ribs, dipping into the curve of my waist, and dragging slowly across the underside of my breast. He watches every reaction, listens for every catch in my breath, every unconscious whimper pulled from my throat. "How adventurous are you, city girl?"

My fingers dig into his shoulders, anchoring myself against the building sensations. "As much as you need me to be."

That does something to him. I feel the shudder in his body. See the sharp flash of heat in his eyes. The restraint in him thins, cracks.

"Good." He leans in, mouth brushing my ear, his voice a rasp that sends lightning straight down my spine. "I'm not soft. I'm not slow. And I'm not going to pretend this is anything less than what it is."

"I know what this is."

He pulls back just enough to meet my gaze head-on, blue eyes gone black with hunger. "So... Do you need a safe word?"

The way he asks it isn't cruel. It's careful. Intentional.

It's a test and a gift.

"Should I?" I draw in a shaking breath. My pulse thrums hard against my throat.

His mouth lifts, just slightly. "I plan on pushing you. And you should know—I'll stop the second you need me to. But if you don't say it..." His thumb drags slowly across my bottom lip, gaze locked on mine. "I won't stop."

Everything tightens.

My body. My breath. The air between us.

I swallow hard, not from fear—but anticipation. And trust.

"Candy cane." The word comes out quiet, steady. "If I need you to stop... I'll say candy cane."

He nods once. Approves. "Say it again. Let me hear it in your voice."

"Candy cane."

A pause. The silence electric.

"Noted." His smile turns wicked. "Now, don't fucking use it."

He kisses me again—deep and claiming—and then he's everywhere. Teeth and tongue, hands gripping, molding, guiding. His body moves over mine with a precision that borders on reverence but never loses that edge of wild intent. When he finally enters me, it's one slow, brutal stroke that leaves me gasping, stretched, filled, and completely undone.

"God, Jackson—"

"Feel that?" he growls, his hips grinding into mine. "This is how I'll take you. All of you. Every time."

The cot creaks beneath us, protesting the rhythm he sets—hard, deep, relentless. His hand slides under my back, lifting my hips to change the angle, and I nearly sob from the pleasure.

He covers me, shields me, fucks me like a man who's

waited too long and doesn't plan to waste a single second. Not with words. Not with movement. Not with me.

And through it all, his eyes never leave mine—refusing to let me hide, or retreat, or come apart in silence.

"Let me hear you, city girl." His voice scrapes along my skin like gravel and silk, dark and dangerous, lips brushing mine with every relentless thrust. "Scream for me. Shake for me. Come for me."

I do.

Once.

Twice.

Each climax rips through me harder than the last, stealing the air from my lungs and sense from my mind. My nails rake down his back. He doesn't flinch. Doesn't slow.

He owns every inch of me.

Jackson rears back just enough to look down, eyes hooded, jaw tight, his hand sliding beneath my thigh and hooking it high around his waist. His thrusts go deeper now. Harder. The stretch borders on pain but never crosses the line. It only sharpens the pleasure and sets me ablaze.

"That's it," he growls against my throat, teeth grazing, breath hot. "You take what I give you. You like it when I take charge."

A whimper breaks from me. I don't even know if it's yes or more or please—because all three are true.

He grabs my wrists and pins them above my head, one big hand locking me in place. His body pounds into mine, claiming me, marking me, making it impossible to think of anything except the ache, the fullness, him.

"Stay with me." His voice drops low, a command more than a plea, hips grinding in a rhythm that steals coherent thought. "Right here. Right now. You're not going anywhere."

My legs tremble, clamping tighter around his waist. The world tilts. Time fractures. My universe becomes the rough drag of his calloused palm down my ribs, the press of his chest to mine, the brutal beauty of his dominance as he pushes me to the brink again.

"You feel that?" he rasps, rolling his hips with lethal control. "That's mine."

He drives in harder. My back arches. The storm outside hammers against the windows, wind howling—but it's nothing compared to the feral sound tearing from my throat when I shatter beneath him.

Jackson's name leaves me in a cry that tastes like surrender. He surges one final time, body tensing, his release pulsing deep inside me. He stays there, chest heaving, face buried in the curve of my neck, his weight a comfort, a claim.

"Mine," he breathes again. Not a question. A truth.

And I don't want to belong to anyone else.

For several heartbeats, neither of us moves. The only sounds are our gradually slowing breaths and the distant howl of the diminishing storm. Jackson's weight should feel crushing, yet it grounds me, preventing me from floating away on the lingering waves of pleasure.

Eventually, he shifts, moving beside me rather than atop me, arms keeping me close in the cot's limited space. The sudden vulnerability of nakedness in the shelter's chill draws me closer to his warmth.

"Are you okay?" His voice is unexpectedly gentle, and his fingers brush the hair from my face with a tenderness that contrasts sharply with the passionate dominance of moments before.

"Better than okay." Words seem inadequate for the lingering glow suffusing my body. "That was..."

"Yeah." His agreement is accompanied by a small smile that

transforms his usually stern features into something beautiful. "It was."

Silence settles between us, not awkward but contemplative. His fingers trace idle patterns on my shoulder, and my hand rests against his chest, feeling the steady rhythm of his heart.

"I don't usually..." His words trail off, with uncharacteristic uncertainty in his tone. "Not since—"

"Emma." The name no longer feels forbidden between us.

He nods, swallowing visibly. "Haven't wanted to. Haven't let myself."

The admission carries weight beyond the obvious meaning —trust implied, barriers lowered, something profound in the simple fact of his surrender to desire.

"Thank you." My fingers trace the line of his jaw, rough with stubble.

His eyebrow lifts questioningly.

"For trusting me with that part of yourself."

Understanding flickers in his eyes—then deepens, softens. Vulnerability ghosts across his expression, a rare crack in the steel. He doesn't speak. Just presses his lips to my forehead, reverent, lingering. And something in me splits open.

The moment stretches. Then snaps.

He takes my mouth like he's starving, hands already sliding under the blanket, yanking me beneath him. No hesitation. No gentleness now. Just hunger. Frenzied. Feral.

The blanket is gone. So are the limits. He shoves me back against the cot, mouth crashing into mine, hands everywhere —ruthless, desperate, claiming.

Outside, the blizzard howls like it wants in.

Inside, he dismantles me piece by piece.

I'm on my knees, arms braced, chest to mattress, hips high. His cock slams into me from behind, deep and merciless, the slap of our bodies drowned only by the wind shrieking through the trees.

Then his hand moves—slow across the curve of my ass. Testing. Teasing.

The first strike lands sharp.

A gasp tears from my throat. My spine arches. My fingers claw the sheets.

He doesn't stop. Another slap. Harder. Then again.

The sting ripples through me—white-hot, pure and perfect. My muscles lock, then melt.

"You love that," he growls behind me, voice shredded with hunger. "Smacking your ass while I fuck you raw."

A fourth strike. Then a fifth. Each one timed between thrusts, brutal percussion that drives me deeper into the mattress. My moans turn shameless—needy, wrecked.

I bite down on a whimper and he laughs—low and wicked.

"That's right. Let it out."

He fucks me harder. Spanks me again.

And again.

By the time he slows, my skin burns and my pussy throbs, stretched tight around him, soaked and trembling.

Then—he pulls out.

A shocked sound slips from me, desperate and wrecked, but before I can speak, I'm weightless.

He lifts me like I weigh nothing.

Spins me.

Tosses me onto the cot with a growl that sounds like it's been waiting years to break free. The mattress groans under the impact, the heat of his body crashing over mine as he shoves my thighs open and covers me with his own.

His mouth claims mine in a brutal kiss—no softness, no mercy. Just teeth, tongue, command.

Then his hand finds my throat. Not choking. Just holding. His fingers tighten.

My breath stutters—and instinctively, my hands fly up to his wrist.

His gaze snaps to mine, wild and blazing.

"No," he growls. He catches both of my wrists in one hand, slams them to the mattress above my head. "Leave them there."

His voice is a command soaked in heat and absolute possession.

My pulse kicks. My body arches. I nod—wordless and wrecked.

Then he pushes inside me again—deep, brutal—his weight crushing into mine, his hand still curled at my throat like a promise I'll never forget.

His thrusts return with purpose—each one harder than the last, driving into me like he's staking a claim. My body jolts with every snap of his hips, breath scraping past parted lips, vision going hazy around the edges.

"Keep your hands there," he growls, his grip tightening just enough to remind me who I belong to.

I moan—helpless, shaking—hips rising to meet his every punishing thrust.

The pressure on my throat. The weight of him over me. The helpless ache between my legs. I've never felt this raw. This open.

My arms burn. My lungs beg. My body worships.

And still—he doesn't let up.

"Look at me," he demands, voice low and lethal. "Eyes on mine while I ruin you."

I obey.

Because I have to.

Because there's no oxygen, no logic, no resistance left in

me—just Jackson. Just his cock pounding into me, his body controlling every inch of mine, his eyes holding me hostage.

"You're going to come for me," he says, his voice a sharp blade in the dark. "But not yet."

My whimper earns me another savage thrust, so deep it knocks the air from my lungs.

"You'll come when I say. Not a second before."

I cry out—needing it, dreading it, falling apart under him.

He releases my throat just long enough to cup my jaw, kiss me like he's starving, like he needs my mouth as much as he needs my body.

Then his hand slides between us—ruthless fingers finding my clit, circling, pressing, building the pressure I've been aching for since the moment he touched me.

I'm so close. So close.

But he stops.

I nearly sob.

I'm wrecked. Shaking. Begging with my eyes.

But he's not done.

"Now you'll take the rest," he says, bracing his hand over my wrists again. "Every thrust. Every second. And you won't come until I own it."

I nod, tears spilling—not from pain. From need.

Because I want to belong to him.

Because right now, I already do.

Jackson's hand clamps over mine, pinning both wrists to the mattress with bruising strength. His other returns to my throat—fingers splayed, not squeezing, just holding. Claiming.

"You want to come?" His breath scorches my cheek, hips never losing their brutal rhythm. "Then you'll fucking earn it."

My mouth parts on a silent cry, body arching, frantic.

He growls—low and lethal—and shifts, angling deeper. His cock slams into a spot that detonates fireworks behind my eyes. My thighs quake. My nails dig into the sheets, desperate for something to hold onto.

But there's nothing but him.

Nothing but the endless assault of pleasure and pain and dominance I can't escape.

He leans down, lips dragging over the shell of my ear.

"Open your eyes."

I try—I do—but they flutter closed again when his thrusts go even harder.

A warning rumble escapes his throat.

"Open. Your. Fucking. Eyes."

I force them wide, vision blurred with tears, every nerve ending lit like a fuse.

"That's it," he snarls. "Watch me. While I break every fucking part of you."

Then, his hand slips between my legs again.

Two fingers. Ruthless pressure. Fast, rough circles that rip a scream from my throat.

I try to twist. Try to hold back.

I can't.

It's too much. Too fast. Too him.

I break.

The orgasm crashes through me, savage and raw, a violent unraveling that shreds me from the inside out. I scream his name, body seizing beneath his, back arching off the bed as wave after wave rolls through me.

Jackson doesn't slow.

Doesn't soften.

He fucks me through it, into it, past it—until I'm sobbing, twitching, clinging to the last thread of reality while he wrings every last ounce of pleasure from my ruined body.

When he comes, it's a growl torn from his chest, hips jerking hard as he empties into me. He holds me down—

pressed, pinned, possessed—every inch of his body screaming ownership.

And then he stills.

The silence crashes in like an aftershock.

I'm limp beneath him. Shattered. Marked.

His.

He doesn't let go. Doesn't speak. Just breathes against my skin, like maybe I broke him, too.

Angel's Peak

CHAPTER 8

UNTIL THE FIRE DIES

WE DON'T STOP.

Not for food. Not for rest. Not even when our limbs tremble from overuse and the room reeks of sweat and sex. The air is heavy—thick with need, raw from breathless moans and the slap of skin on skin.

He takes me again and again, each time rougher. Possessive. Each time, stripping away more of what I was before him.

He grabs me by the throat, dragging my back against the log wall. His hand fists in my hair. Yanks. A growl tears from his throat.

"Up."

He lifts me in one brutal movement, thighs catching around his hips. His cock slams in—fast, punishing, devastating.

I cry out, fingers clawing at his shoulders, at air, at anything I can find as my back scrapes bark. He fucks me with purpose. With fury. With a promise I feel in my bones: *You're mine.*

When I come, it's with my face buried against his neck, teeth sinking into his shoulder to muffle the scream.

Later—much later—he lays me out on the cot again. The fire throws gold across the walls. My legs are weak. My pulse thunders.

This time, he kisses me slowly. Deep. Fingers threading through my hair as his mouth claims mine with aching tenderness. I moan into it, ready to give him anything.

But he pulls back.

Eyes sharp. Calculating. Dominant.

"Get on your knees."

The word cracks through the space like thunder. I blink up at him, heart hammering. My body aches in all the right places. My lips are swollen. My thighs bruised. But his voice makes me throb all over again.

He doesn't move. Doesn't push.

He just waits.

I hesitate.

A beat.

His gaze narrows—slow. Patient. Merciless. "That wasn't a request," he says, voice like dark velvet. "On your knees."

The command pulses through me like heat. But still... I hesitate. Not because I don't want to obey—but because I do. Too much.

His hand brushes the side of my face. Gentle. Reverent.

"Unless you're going to say your safe word," he says, low and firm, "you'll get on your knees and put your mouth where it belongs."

The breath leaves me in a shudder. Every inch of me tightens.

I drop.

He groans—low, wrecked, and glorious.

His cock is hard, thick, already waiting. I wrap my lips around the head, tongue swirling, eyes locked on his as I sink down. His hand threads into my hair, not forcing, just holding. Guiding.

I suck him slow at first—long, deep drags designed to undo him.

But he wants more.

And I give it.

Gagging. Drooling. Desperate to please.

He fucks my mouth with the same brutal grace he gives everything else—his body. His dominance. His fucking soul.

When he comes, it's with a growl of my name and a thrust so deep I feel it down my throat. I take it all. Every drop. Every shudder. Every breath.

Still later—when our bodies are wrecked and our skin is flushed and raw—he spreads a wool blanket by the fire and lays me across it like something sacred.

The glow paints his chest in gold as he sinks between my thighs, slow and reverent now. His fingers trail over every bruise he's left. Every scratch. Every place his hands claimed me.

And then he slides into me.

Long. Deep. Like worship.

He doesn't speak. Doesn't taunt or tease.

He just moves—slow, deliberate, endless.

His hand cups my jaw, thumb stroking my cheek as he fucks me like he's memorizing every sigh, every flutter of muscle, every gasping breath.

Outside, the snow keeps falling.

Thick. Endless.

Inside, so do we.

Again. And again. And again.

The outside world could be ending, and I wouldn't care.

Not with his mouth on my skin, his body over mine, in mine—claiming me again and again until I can't tell where he ends and I begin.

Time ceases to matter.

Hours pass in a haze of heat and hunger, our bodies tangled in sweat-slick sheets and breathless moans. Afternoon bleeds into evening, the fire crackling low, casting flickering shadows across our skin.

We drift—sometimes into sleep, sometimes into whispered conversation—but we always return to each other. Drawn like gravity. Like obsession.

And each time he takes me, he takes more.

His hands grow rougher. His commands, sharper. He binds my wrists with the tie from his flannel shirt and drapes me over his thigh, spanking me until my cries fill the room—pain blooming into pleasure that makes me writhe.

He doesn't stop when I beg.

He only pauses long enough to trace the red marks on my ass with reverence, then flips me onto my back and fucks me with bruising force, one hand pinning both wrists overhead, the other wrapped tight around my throat.

"You love when I control you," he growls, teeth grazing the shell of my ear. I can only nod, because it's true. No use denying what he can clearly see. "You have no fucking idea what that does to me, knowing you belong to me."

The words splinter me. I arch into him and fall harder.

He tests every limit I never knew I had. Every dark want I never dared name.

He pushes me to the edge, holds me there, and when I think I can't take any more—he gives me more.

There's no room for doubt or shame in his arms. Only heat. Only command. Only the way he fucks me like he's imprinting himself into every nerve, every breath, every broken, blissed-out sound I make.

And through it all—I let him.

Because in his hands, surrender feels like salvation, and I feel worshipped.

Ruined.

Remade.

And I never want it to end.

We remain entwined as afternoon stretches toward evening, drifting in and out of sleep, conversation, and renewed exploration. The shelter's confines no longer feel restrictive but rather intimate, a world unto ourselves where reality can't intrude.

Until it does.

The hand-crank radio on the shelf crackles suddenly to life, its automated weather alert cutting through our private sanctuary.

"Weather advisory update for Angel's Peak region. Storm system moving east, clearing expected by tomorrow afternoon. Temperature rise predicted. Travel advisories remain in effect for backcountry areas. Next update at 0600."

Reality crashes back with the mechanical voice. *Tomorrow.* Clearing. The bubble of our isolation prepares to burst.

Jackson's arms tighten slightly around me, his chest rising with a deep breath against my cheek. Neither of us speaks immediately, the implications hanging heavy between us.

Tomorrow means descent. Returning to Angel's Peak. To separate rooms, separate lives. To the article I came to write, and the mountain he never leaves.

"We should eat something." Jackson's voice breaks the silence, practical concerns reasserting themselves. "Conserve strength for tomorrow."

"Right." The word tastes hollow as I disentangle myself from his warmth, immediately missing the connection.

We dress in silence, the easy intimacy of moments before replaced by something more complicated. Not regret—at least not on my part. But there's no way to avoid our impending separation.

This must end.

Jackson moves to the woodstove, heating a can of stew. His back presents an unreadable canvas, muscles shifting beneath his thermal shirt.

"So." My voice breaks the growing silence. "Tomorrow."

"Looks like it." He doesn't turn; he focuses on the simple task before him.

"Back to reality."

"Back to your article." Now he glances over his shoulder, expression carefully neutral. "Got what you needed?"

"For the article? More than enough." The question carries double meaning, intentional or not. "With you...not nearly."

He nods once, returning his attention to our meal.

His silence reveals nothing of his thoughts regarding what transpired between us—whether it was merely stress relief or something more significant. Pride prevents me from asking outright, from appearing to need reassurance that what we shared mattered.

I can't because we agreed upfront. This was never meant to last.

We eat in relative silence, with occasional comments about practical matters—the descent path, weather considerations, and the estimated time to reach the town. Conversation that carefully avoids addressing the shift in our relationship and the uncertain territory ahead.

Night falls early, hastened by storm clouds still lingering above. The shelter grows colder with sunset, necessitating closer proximity around the woodstove once more.

Jackson arranges blankets near the heat source, and our sleeping area from the previous night is now laden with new significance. When he holds the blanket open in invitation, I join him without hesitation, our bodies fitting together with newly familiar ease.

His arm wraps around my waist, pulling me against the

solid warmth of his chest. My head finds its place naturally beneath his chin, ear pressed to his steady heartbeat.

"Jackson?" My voice emerges softly in the darkness.

"Hm?" The sound rumbles through his chest against my cheek.

"What happens when we reach town?"

The question hangs between us, unavoidable now. His breathing changes slightly, the only indication that the query affects him.

"You leave and write your article." His voice reveals nothing.

"And you?"

"I stay. Guide. Rescue foolish writers who ignore storm warnings."

The attempt at lightness falls flat, inadequate against the weight of what's developed between us. My fingers curl against his chest, seeking anchorage against the approaching separation.

"That's it?" The words emerge more vulnerable than intended.

"We agreed." Jackson's hand finds mine, fingers intertwining. "What else can there be?"

No answer presents itself—not one that doesn't sound naive or desperate. We exist in different worlds, our lives running on tracks that were never meant to converge beyond this temporary intersection.

"Nothing, I guess." The words taste like ash. I don't meet his eyes. Can't. Because if I do, I'll crumble.

"We knew this going in." His arms tighten. Just a fraction. Just enough to betray him.

Silence stretches between us, taut as a wire, humming with everything we're trying not to say. We're pretending the world won't crack open in the morning. That goodbye won't taste like blood.

But I can't leave it like this.

I shift. Slowly. Carefully. Letting the sheet fall away as I rise above him, straddle his hips, thighs framing the solid warmth of his body.

His breath catches, eyes locking with mine. No words. No resistance. Just the quiet throb of disbelief as I reach down and guide him inside me.

There's no rush.

I sink onto him with aching precision, the stretch familiar now. Welcome. My palms settle on his chest. His hands grasp my hips, but there's no force behind the grip—just reverence. His eyes never leave mine.

I start to move. Slow. Purposeful. Rolling my hips in languid circles, chasing something deeper than climax. Etching the memory of him into my body, one stroke at a time.

Jackson's throat works around a groan, eyes dark with something unspoken. He holds me as if I might vanish. Like I'm already a ghost he's trying to memorize.

My fingers trace the curve of his jaw, the scar just beneath his bottom lip. I lean down, kiss the hollow of his throat. Taste the salt of our sweat. Hear the stutter in his breath when I clench around him.

"I don't want to let this go," I whisper against his skin.

He slides one hand up my spine, holds me there, forehead against mine, breath mingling as I move—gentle now, deep and steady, like a promise neither of us dares to make out loud.

"Neither do I."

The storm still rages outside. But in here, it's all hush and heat. The quiet rhythm of two people clinging to a lie they both want to rewrite.

And when I fall, I do it with my eyes open. Watching his face. Feeling every inch of him as he follows me over the edge, gasping my name like it means more than either of us will admit.

After, I stay on top of him. His arms curl around me, drawing me down until our hearts beat against each other's chests. Slower now. But not steadier.

Just before sleep pulls me under, his lips find my ear.

"I wish things were different."

This time, I believe him, but I also know that it doesn't change a damn thing.

The confession lingers in the darkness, offering no solutions but acknowledging what neither can deny—that something significant has ignited between us, something neither expected nor sought, yet neither can dismiss as mere physical release.

Tomorrow, we descend the mountain, leaving behind not just this shelter but also the secluded world we created—a world where two damaged people found unexpected healing in each other's arms, where past traumas momentarily receded, where connection transcended boundaries of sensibility and circumstance.

Tomorrow, reality awaits. But tonight, we burn in the darkness, clinging to fantasies we know won't survive beyond these stone walls.

Angel's Peak

CHAPTER 9

DESCENT

SUNLIGHT STREAMS THROUGH THE FROST-RIMMED window, illuminating dust motes dancing in golden beams. After days of relentless gray, the brightness feels almost intrusive, harsh in its clarity.

The storm has broken.

Jackson stands by the window, surveying the transformed landscape outside. His profile cuts a sharp silhouette against the brilliant white world beyond the glass, features set in that familiar mask of professional detachment.

"Clear skies." He speaks to the window rather than to me. "Wind's died down. Temperature's rising."

The words hang in the shelter's still air, their implication unmistakable. It's time to leave.

Our cocoon of isolation, with its intensities and revelations, must be abandoned. Reality beckons from the base of the mountain—my article, his guiding business, the separate lives temporarily entwined by circumstance and chemistry.

Sleep-warmed blankets pool around my waist as I sit on the cot. Cold air nips at my exposed skin despite the sunlight, raising goosebumps along my arms. Jackson turned away during this small vulnerability, offering privacy where none has existed for days. The consideration feels oddly painful after the intimacies we've shared.

"How soon can we head down?" My voice emerges steadier than expected.

"Noon." He moves to the woodstove, stoking the dying embers without looking my way. "Need to pack supplies, check conditions along the route first."

The awkwardness between us settles like a physical presence, taking up space in the small shelter. Last night's whispered wish—"I wish things were different"—hovers unacknowledged in daylight.

Breakfast consists of the last protein bars, consumed in silence punctuated only by the occasional crackle from the woodstove. Jackson packs methodically, equipment disappearing into his backpack—rope, emergency supplies, the half-empty first aid kit.

"You'll need to wear this." He finally approaches, holding out climbing gear—a harness similar to the one used in my rescue. "Snow's unstable after the storm. High avalanche risk."

Our fingers brush during the exchange, and the brief contact sends electricity up my arm despite everything. Jackson quickly withdraws, turning back to his preparations.

"I'll need to secure you to my line." His voice remains professional and impersonal. "Whole mountain's a death trap right now for solo hikers."

"I won't argue this time." A weak attempt at lightening the mood.

The ghost of a smile touches his lips before vanishing. "Smart woman."

The praise shouldn't affect me, yet warmth blooms in my chest regardless. Pathetic how eagerly my heart responds to the smallest crumb of approval from this man.

By mid-morning, preparations are complete. The shelter

stands ready for its next emergency occupant—wood stacked, supplies organized, surfaces wiped clean of our presence. Only memories remain as evidence of what transpired within these stone walls.

Jackson steps outside first, scanning the terrain. I follow into blinding brightness. The sun's reflection off pristine snow momentarily overwhelms me after days in the shelter's dim interior.

The world has transformed into a breathtaking winter wonderland—snow blankets every surface in crystalline perfection; icicles hang from rock outcroppings like nature's chandeliers, and the sky stretches into endless blue above—beauty disguised as deadly danger, much like the man standing beside me.

"Stay close." Jackson secures the shelter door, locking away our temporary sanctuary. "Step exactly where I step. Touch nothing without asking first."

He approaches with the climbing harness, kneeling to help me into it. His hands move with professional efficiency, adjusting straps with precision, but something has changed. The fingers that checked my buckles tremble slightly, barely perceptible but unmistakable to someone who knows the steady certainty of those hands.

"Too tight?" His voice betrays nothing, eyes focused on equipment rather than my face.

"It's fine."

Jackson double-checks each connection, tugging testing straps that are already secure. The caution might seem excessive to an observer, but understanding dawns with painful clarity—he's replaying Emma's accident, determined not to repeat history.

"Ready?" He finally meets my gaze, eyes the color of glacier ice reflecting the brilliant sky.

"As I'll ever be."

The journey begins in a single file, Jackson breaking trail through snow that reaches mid-thigh in places. A climbing rope connects us, five feet of tether keeping me physically linked to him while my emotional distance grows with each careful step.

The descent proves more challenging than anticipated. What appeared to be gentle slopes reveal treacherous drops beneath deceptive snow blankets. Ice-glazed rocks lurk under innocent-looking powder. The mountain, beautiful in its winter dress, conceals deadly traps with seductive beauty.

Jackson remains hyper-vigilant, constantly glancing back, adjusting our course to avoid hidden dangers, never allowing me beyond arm's reach. When a snow shelf suddenly gives way beneath my boot, his reaction comes with lightning speed—hand shooting out to grasp my jacket, yanking me against his solid frame before I can fully register the danger.

For one breathless moment, we stand pressed together; his arm iron-tight around my waist, his heartbeat thundering against my back. Then, as quickly as it happened, he sets me upright, professional distance reinstated.

"Careful." The single word emerges rough-edged, revealing more than he likely intended.

The descent continues in this pattern—careful steps, occasional corrections, brief moments of physical contact that spark memories of intimacy now wrapped in professional necessity.

Around us, the mountain reveals its grandeur in ways impossible to appreciate during the blizzard. Like ancient giants wearing ermine cloaks, massive rock formations are draped in snow. Pine trees bent beneath white burdens, creating natural archways across sections of our path. In one clearing, sunlight refracts through ice crystals hanging from branches, casting rainbow prisms across undisturbed snow.

"It's beautiful." The words escape in a cloud of breath, inadequate against such majesty.

Jackson pauses, following my gaze across the vista where mountains stretch to the horizon, their peaks piercing the cobalt sky. "Worth writing about?"

"Beyond words." The honesty slips out unbidden. "Though I'll have to try anyway."

Something softens in his expression—a brief glimpse of the man from the shelter rather than the professional guide. "You'll do it justice."

The compliment warms despite the chill air. We continue downward, and the terrain gradually becomes less severe as elevation decreases. Trees grow more plentiful, offering occasional shelter from the brilliant sun that has begun transforming the snow surface from powder to slush.

Midway down, Jackson calls for a rest. We perch on a fallen log cleared of snow, water bottles passing between gloved hands, and energy bars providing necessary fuel. The silence between us has evolved from awkward to something more companionable, though the undercurrent of unspoken feelings remains.

"Will you mention me?" His question catches me off-guard. "In your article."

The vulnerability behind the query tugs at something deep within my chest. "Do you want me to?"

Jackson considers this, gaze fixed on the distant peaks. "Not the personal stuff. But the mountain safety aspects— maybe someone will listen to your experience better than my warnings."

"I'll make you sound properly intimidating and all-knowing." A smile tugs at my lips. "The Mountain King of Angel's Peak."

His laugh surprises us both—short but genuine, transforming his stern features into something breathtaking. "God, please don't."

"Mountain Guardian? Alpine Sentinel? Wilderness Wizard?"

"Stop." But amusement lingers in his eyes, a precious glimpse of what might have been under different circumstances.

The moment passes too quickly. Jackson's professional demeanor returns as he checks his watch and surveys our remaining route. "I need to keep moving. I want to reach the base cabin before the afternoon melt makes conditions worse."

Back on our feet, the descent continues, each step bringing us closer to separation. As we drop in elevation, the snow thins, patches of exposed ground appearing with increasing frequency. The world gradually becomes less white, less pristine, and less isolated.

Jackson's base cabin appears around a bend in the trail—a substantially larger structure than the emergency shelter. It is constructed of sturdy logs with a metal roof currently shedding snow in slow-motion avalanches. Solar panels glint on the south-facing slope, a satellite dish nestled discreetly among them. This is a place where wilderness meets civilization in careful balance.

"Home sweet home." Jackson's voice carries no inflection as he unlocks the heavy wooden door.

Stepping inside feels like entering another world after days in the primitive shelter. Polished wooden floors stretch beneath boots that suddenly seem inappropriately snow-covered. A river stone fireplace dominates one wall, unlit but immaculately maintained. Modern appliances gleam in a compact kitchen. Comfortable furniture is arranged for both function and comfort. Books line built-in shelves—field guides, climbing manuals, classic literature.

Civilization strikes like a physical force—jarring and

almost overwhelming after our primitive existence. The contrast highlights how far we've traveled physically and emotionally in four short days.

Jackson moves with the ease of long familiarity, stowing gear, checking thermostats, and performing the routine of homecoming. I stand awkwardly in the entry, suddenly uncertain of my place in this new context.

"You can put your things there." He gestures toward a bench clearly designed for shedding outdoor gear. "Bathroom's through that door if you want to clean up."

The hot water feels miraculous against skin that's known nothing but melted snow and cold-water sponge baths for days. Standing under the shower's steady stream, I finally acknowledge what I've been suppressing since waking—heartache.

Not dramatic, soul-crushing pain, but a quieter, more insidious ache of possibility lost before it could fully form.

Ridiculous to mourn something that never truly existed beyond a temporary bubble of intense physical attraction. Yet the feeling persists, settling behind my ribs like a small, cold stone.

Dressed again in clothes that smell of woodsmoke and mountain, I emerge to find Jackson in the kitchen, phone to his ear. The sight startles—technology reconnecting us to the wider world, another tether to reality.

"Yes, both safe. No injuries beyond her sprained ankle. Much better now." His eyes meet mine across the room, expression unreadable. "About an hour, depending on road conditions. Will do."

He sets the phone down, something shifting in his demeanor—a return to the reserved mountain guide I first encountered in the diner, professional mask firmly in place.

"That was the sheriff. Your hotel's been worried. Roads are clear enough to get you back to town." He busies himself collecting keys from a hook by the door. "Need to check some equipment first, then I'll drive you."

The statement lands with finality—our adventure concluding in mundane transportation arrangements and concerned innkeepers. The contrast between this ordinary ending and the extraordinary connection we forged feels almost surreal.

Jackson disappears into what appears to be a gear room, leaving me with the echo of what's ending. My article still needs completion, and our professional obligations wait for us regardless of our personal complications.

Thirty minutes pass before Jackson reemerges, keys jingling in his hand. "Ready?"

The drive to town passes largely in silence, broken only by occasional commentary about landmarks visible through freshly plowed roads. Angel's Peak appears around a bend—quaint buildings emerge from snow banks, smoke rises from chimneys, and life continues as if nothing extraordinary happened on the mountain above.

We pull up outside Mabel's Guesthouse, my temporary home before the shelter became our world. The transition feels impossibly abrupt—from an intimate connection to an awkward goodbye in the space of a four-mile drive.

"Thank you." The words encompass everything and nothing. "For the rescue. The shelter... Everything."

Jackson's hands remain on the steering wheel, knuckles white with tension. "Just doing my job."

The dismissal stings despite its obvious falsehood. "Right. The job."

Silence stretches between us, heavy with unspoken words. Finally, he turns slightly, profile sharp against the afternoon light. "How long will you stay? In town."

"Three more days." Hope flutters unwelcome in my chest.

"I need to finish the interviews and take some photos of the trails. When weather permits."

He nods once, gaze fixed forward again. "Good luck with the article."

The dismissal lies beneath professional courtesy. This is goodbye.

Pride straightens my spine as I reach for the door handle. "Goodbye, Jackson."

No response comes as I exit the vehicle, collecting my backpack from the rear seat. Only when I reach the guesthouse steps does his window lower, voice carrying across the crisp air.

"Cloe." My name in his mouth still sends shivers down my spine. "Be careful out there."

Before I can respond, the window rises, the engine revs, and Jackson Hart disappears around the corner, leaving me standing in the snow with a heart full of words I never got to say.

Mabel greets me with effusive concern and endless questions that receive carefully edited answers. The hot bath and real food she insists upon should feel like luxuries after days of survival, yet something essential seems missing despite the comforts.

By evening, professional instincts reassert themselves. My laptop hums to life, fingers finding keyboard rhythm as I shape the article that brought me to Angel's Peak. The words flow surprisingly quickly, the experience still raw enough to translate into vivid prose.

Yet something nags beneath the writing—questions unanswered, story incomplete. After two hours of productive work, restlessness drives me from my room to the town's single bar, The Pickaxe, where locals gather nightly.

"Well, look who survived!" Darlene from the diner spots

me immediately, waving from behind the bar where she apparently moonlights. "Hart got you down in one piece, I see."

The diner waitress's presence in this new context momentarily disorients me until I remember—small town, multiple jobs, everyone knowing everyone's business.

"He did." Settling onto a barstool feels strangely normal after days of extraordinary circumstances. "Very professional."

"That's our Jackson." Darlene slides a glass of amber liquid before me without asking. "On the house. Mountain rescue special."

The whiskey burns pleasantly, warming paths through my chest. Around me, locals cast curious glances, whispers barely disguised behind raised glasses. The outsider who needed rescuing—now the subject of hometown gossip.

"Working on your article?" Darlene wipes the already clean counter with practiced movements. "About our little slice of heaven?"

"Among other things." The opening presents itself naturally. "Actually, I'm curious about the town's history with mountain rescue. Jackson mentioned his grandfather started the first team?"

Darlene's face lights with local pride. "Old Man Hart was a legend around here. Taught Jackson everything he knows about these mountains."

The conversation flows from there—stories of dramatic rescues, the Hart family's three generations of mountain guides, the respect bordering on reverence that locals hold for their wilderness protectors.

"Jackson's the best we've ever had." The ranger from the diner joins the conversation, settling onto the neighboring stool. "Could've gone pro anywhere—had offers from major expedition companies. Everest, K2, you name it."

"Why didn't he?" The question emerges more personally invested than professionally curious.

Their exchanged glance speaks volumes.

"Emma." Darlene's voice drops. "They were planning to move after the wedding. She'd gotten some research grant in Colorado. Then the accident happened and..." She trails off, shaking her head.

"He changed." The ranger continues where she left off. "Shut down completely for months. When he came back, he was different. Focused. Obsessive about safety. Never leaves the mountain except for supplies."

"Hasn't been with anyone since." Darlene adds, then flushes slightly. "Not that we gossip or anything."

The information shouldn't affect me as it does, shouldn't twist something painful beneath my ribs. What happened in the shelter was an anomaly for him—an exception to three years of self-imposed isolation.

"Brilliant guide," the ranger concludes, "but a broken man. Mountain took something from him."

The conversation shifts to other topics, but their assessment echoes in my mind long after I return to the guesthouse. Jackson Hart—brilliant but broken, capable of saving others but unwilling to save himself.

As I prepare for bed in a room that feels too large, too quiet, too empty after days of shared space and body heat, their words continue to resonate. The man I glimpsed beneath the professional guide's exterior—the one who laughed at my ridiculous nickname suggestions, who trembled slightly when securing my harness, who whispered impossible wishes in darkness—remains trapped on that mountain, perhaps as surely as we were trapped by the storm.

The realization settles with unexpected weight: the most treacherous part of my Angel's Peak adventure wasn't the blizzard, the cliff face, or even the isolation.

It was falling for a man who gave his heart to these mountains long ago—and has no intention of ever taking it back.

Angel's Peak

CHAPTER 10

TREACHEROUS PATH

MORNING SUNLIGHT STREAMS THROUGH LACE curtains, casting delicate patterns across my laptop screen. Two days back in civilization, and the article is taking shape— the wilderness beauty, the danger of underestimating nature, the practical safety tips distilled from Jackson's teachings. Everything except the story beneath the story.

My phone vibrates against the antique writing desk, my editor's name flashing on the screen.

"This is good, Matthews." Diane's voice crackles through the connection, New York bustle audible in the background. "But we need more."

My stomach tightens. "More what?"

"The human element. You survived four days in a blizzard with Angel's Peak's legendary mountain man. There's gold there."

"He's a private person." My fingers trace the edge of the laptop, remembering callused hands against my skin. "I promised discretion."

"I'm not asking for his medical records." Keys clack as she presumably scrolls through my draft. "But readers connect with people, not landscapes. You've got the reclusive hero who saved your life. That's the hook."

"It's exploitative." The defense rises automatically.

"It's journalism." Diane's tone sharpens. "Look, get me something on Hart—his philosophy, his connection to the mountain, anything. Or this stays a pretty nature piece buried in the back pages."

The threat hangs between us—my breakthrough opportunity dissolving into yet another forgettable article.

"I'll see what I can do." The words taste bitter.

"Good. Revised draft by tomorrow." The call ends with a decisive click.

Rain begins to tap against the window, matching my darkening mood. The ethical dilemma stretches before me—betray Jackson's trust for career advancement, or honor his privacy at professional cost.

No contest, really. Some lines shouldn't be crossed.

Standing at the window, watching raindrops chase each other down the glass, movement catches my attention. A familiar truck crawls past the guesthouse, slowing almost imperceptibly before continuing down the street.

Jackson.

My heart stutters against my ribs, an unwelcome reminder of feelings I've been working to suppress. What is he doing here, in town, passing my temporary home?

Before reason can intervene, I grab my jacket and notebook—a journalist's armor—and head into the gentle rain. Professional pretense. That's all this is.

The walk to Jackson's base cabin takes forty minutes, enough time for doubt to build with each step. The rain intensifies, soaking through my inadequate jacket and plastering my hair to my forehead. By the time his property comes into view, rationality has almost won.

Then I spot his truck in the driveway, recently arrived

judging by the water still dripping from its frame. He's here. The knowledge propels me forward before courage can fail.

The wooden steps creak beneath my weight, announcing my presence before my knuckles can meet the door. Three sharp knocks echo in the afternoon quiet, followed by heavy silence.

Just as I'm considering retreat, the door opens—barely enough to reveal Jackson's face, surprise quickly masked by carefully constructed neutrality.

"Cloe." My name emerges flat, a statement rather than greeting.

Rain drips from my hair onto my already-soaked shoulders. "Can I come in?"

His hesitation speaks volumes, but mountain hospitality apparently outweighs personal reluctance. The door widens grudgingly, revealing Jackson in worn jeans and a flannel shirt, sleeves rolled to expose forearms corded with muscle. The domestic setting strikes me oddly—this man of wilderness framed by kitchen counters and bookshelves.

"You're soaked." He disappears briefly, returning with a towel that he offers without touching my hand.

"Thanks." The terry cloth smells like him—pine and something clean, masculine.

The cabin feels different in daylight—warmer and more lived-in than during our brief post-rescue stop. Climbing guides line bookshelves alongside dog-eared classics. Coffee rings stain the handcrafted table. A half-completed crossword puzzle lies abandoned beside an ancient leather armchair—evidence of a solitary but not austere existence.

"What brings you up the mountain in this?" Jackson gestures toward the window where rain continues its persistent assault.

A dozen potential answers race through my mind—the

article, closure, simple curiosity. None quite reach the truth lurking beneath.

"I saw your truck." The words emerge before I can censor them. "Passing the guesthouse."

Something flickers across his features—discomfort, perhaps embarrassment at being caught. "Supply run to town."

"The guesthouse isn't on the route to the supply store."

His jaw tightens, and a familiar tension gathers in his shoulders. "What do you want, Cloe?"

Direct. Unavoidable. Typical Jackson.

"Clarity, maybe." My fingers twist the damp towel. "My editor wants more for the article. About you."

His expression shutters immediately. "We've been through this."

"I'm not asking for permission." My chin lifts slightly. "I'm telling you, I refused."

Surprise registers briefly before suspicion returns. "Why?"

"Because some things matter more than career advancement." The newspaper resting on his kitchen counter catches my attention—open to an article about backcountry safety. "Like privacy. Like promises."

Jackson's posture shifts subtly, wariness giving way to something less defensive. He moves to the kitchen, filling a kettle with practiced movements. "You should warm up."

The tentative peace offering hangs between us. I nod, shrugging off my wet jacket, draping it carefully over a chair by the woodstove.

Silence stretches as he prepares tea, his back deliberately turned. The domestic normalcy of the scene contrasts sharply with the undercurrent of tension vibrating between us. My eyes track him involuntarily, memory overlaying the present —those hands on my body, those shoulders beneath my fingers.

"Why did you drive past the guesthouse?" The question emerges softer than intended.

The kettle whistles, shrill in the weighted silence. He takes his time answering, pouring steaming water into mugs and adding tea bags with deliberate focus.

"Because I wanted to see you." The admission emerges rough-edged, reluctant. "And didn't want to see you. Both."

The honesty disarms me more effectively than any evasion could have. Jackson turns, extending a mug without quite meeting my eyes.

"I get it." My fingers brush his during the exchange, sending unwelcome warmth up my arm. "I've been writing a paragraph about snowpack conditions for two hours because it keeps me from writing about you."

Something almost like a smile touches his mouth before disappearing. "How's the article coming otherwise?"

"Good. Almost done." The tea burns sweet and strong on my tongue. "Just missing the element my editor insists will make it cover-worthy."

"Which is?"

"The mysterious mountain guide with the tragic past and hero complex." The attempt at lightness falls flat. "Her words, not mine."

Jackson's expression darkens. "Using me to sell magazines."

"I told her no." My voice rises slightly. "Why do you immediately assume the worst?"

"Experience." He sets his mug down with unnecessary force. "Everyone wants something."

"Not everything is transactional, Jackson." Irritation flares, hot and sudden. "Some people just care."

"About a man they knew for four days?" Skepticism drips from every word.

"Four days of survival. Intimacy. Honesty." Each word emerges sharper than the last. "Or was that all transactional, too? My body in exchange for warmth? My story for your protection?"

His eyes narrow dangerously. "That's not what happened."

"Isn't it? Because you've made it pretty clear that's all it could ever be." The hurt I've been suppressing bubbles up, acidic and undeniable. "God forbid you actually feel something genuine again. Much easier to hide behind Emma's ghost."

The moment the words leave my mouth, I regret them. Jackson's face transforms, pain flashing raw before iron control slams down.

"You don't know what you're talking about." His voice drops to something dangerous, quiet.

"Don't I?" Something reckless drives me forward, closing the distance between us. "I know you're using guilt as a shield. I know you're punishing yourself by refusing to live fully. I know you felt something real in that shelter, something that scared you more than any blizzard."

His breathing changes, becomes measured and controlled. "You should go."

"Why? Because I'm right?" Another step closer, close enough to catch his scent, to feel the heat radiating from his body. "Or because you drove past my hotel today wondering what if?"

"Stop." The word emerges strained, a warning.

"Make me." My palms connect with his chest, a gentle shove born of frustration rather than anger.

His hand catches my wrist—not roughly, just enough to halt the movement. Electricity crackles between us, familiar and dangerous. His eyes drop to my lips for the briefest moment, pupils dilating slightly.

The air thickens, every breath suddenly requiring effort. My chest rises and falls rapidly, matching his increasingly uneven breathing.

"Tell me you didn't think about it." My voice drops to barely above a whisper. "About me. After."

Jackson's response comes in motion rather than words—his free hand sliding behind my neck, fingers tangling in my damp hair, pulling me toward him with unmistakable intent.

Our mouths collide with none of the tentative exploration of our first real kiss. This is hunger, frustration, and days of emptiness seeking fulfillment. His lips move against mine with desperate intensity, tongue demanding entrance I eagerly grant.

My hands fist in his shirt, pulling him closer, needing to eliminate any space between us. Jackson responds by walking me backward until my spine meets the wall, his body pressing against mine with delicious weight.

The kiss deepens and transforms, anger melting into something equally powerful but infinitely sweeter. His hands frame my face with surprising gentleness, thumbs stroking my cheekbones even as his mouth devours mine.

"This changes nothing," he murmurs against my lips, the words contradicted by the reverence in his touch.

"I know." My fingers work at his shirt buttons, needing to feel his skin beneath my palms. "I don't care."

Clothing becomes an unwelcome barrier, removed in urgent, ungraceful movements. His flannel shirt falls to the floor, and my sweater follows moments later. The contrast between the cool wall at my back and Jackson's burning skin against my front sends shivers racing along my nerves.

His mouth traces a path along my jaw, down my neck, finding sensitive places remembered from our night in the shelter. My head falls back against the wall, offering greater access, surrendering to sensation.

"Not here." Jackson's voice emerges rough against my collarbone. "Not like this."

Before I can protest, he lifts me, hands secure beneath my

thighs as my legs wrap instinctively around his waist. The display of strength sends heat pooling low in my abdomen as he carries me toward the bedroom.

Unlike the utilitarian shelter cot, Jackson's bed welcomes us with soft flannel sheets and a handmade quilt that's hastily pushed aside. He lays me down with surprising care before covering my body with his own, weight supported on forearms braced beside my head.

"Last chance to walk away." His eyes search mine, offering an escape I have no intention of taking.

My answer comes in action rather than words, pulling him down for another kiss that erases any remaining doubt. What follows transcends our shelter encounter—less desperate but somehow more intense. Each touch carries meaning beyond physical pleasure, and each kiss communicates what words cannot.

Jackson's protective nature emerges in how thoroughly he ensures my satisfaction before seeking his own, in the careful attention he pays to every response, in whispered questions making certain of consent despite my obvious enthusiasm.

When we finally join, the sensation overwhelms me—fullness, connection, and vulnerability beyond anything experienced in the shelter. My name falls from his lips like a prayer. His movements are controlled yet increasingly urgent as pleasure builds between us.

My release comes with stunning intensity, Jackson's name torn from my throat as waves of sensation wash through me. He follows moments later, face buried against my neck, body tensing before relaxing into boneless weight above me.

For several heartbeats, neither of us moves. The only sounds are our gradually slowing breaths and the persistent patter of rain against the windows. Jackson's weight should feel crushing, yet it grounds me, preventing me from floating away on lingering waves of pleasure.

Eventually, he shifts, moving beside me rather than atop me, one arm keeping me close to his side. My fingers trace idle patterns across his chest, finding the scar I remember from before, following its path across his ribs.

"This still doesn't change anything, does it?" The question emerges quiet but clear in the room's stillness.

Jackson's breathing changes slightly, the only indication that the query affects him. His silence provides answer enough.

"I thought so." My finger continues its path across his skin, memorizing textures I'll soon leave behind.

"It's not that simple." His voice rumbles beneath my ear.

"It never is." Rolling to my side, I face him directly. "But sometimes we make things more complicated than they need to be."

His expression shifts, and something like regret crosses his features before disappearing behind careful neutrality. "You have a life waiting in Burlington."

"And you have one here." Completing the familiar argument. "With your ghosts and your mountains."

"Cloe—"

"It's okay." The lie tastes bitter but necessary. "I knew what this was. What it wasn't."

The acceptance costs more than it should for someone who claims to want nothing beyond the physical. Carefully extracting myself from his embrace, I sit, suddenly aware of my nakedness in more ways than one.

"I should go." The words emerge steadier than expected.

Jackson doesn't contradict me, doesn't ask me to stay. He just watches with that unreadable expression as I collect scattered clothing, rebuilding my armor piece by piece.

Dressed again, I pause at the bedroom doorway, unwilling to leave without closure or acknowledgment of what transpired between us.

"For what it's worth, you should know something." My fingers grip the doorframe for support. "I won't use you for my article. Not because you asked, but because some stories aren't meant for public consumption. This one's just ours."

Something shifts in his expression—surprise, perhaps gratitude. "Thank you."

The simple acknowledgment will have to suffice. With a final nod, I move through the cabin, collecting my still-damp jacket from beside the woodstove.

Jackson follows, maintaining a careful distance. At the front door, hesitation grips me—the knowledge that crossing this threshold likely means ending whatever tenuous connection we've formed.

His hand catches mine as I reach for the doorknob, the touch sending familiar electricity racing up my arm. For one breathless moment, hope flares—foolish, stubborn hope that perhaps he'll ask me to stay and suggest some impossible compromise.

Instead, he lifts my hand to his lips, pressing a kiss against my knuckles with heartbreaking gentleness. "Be safe out there, city girl."

The nickname, laced with affection he won't directly express, nearly undoes my composure. With a final nod, I step into the rain, letting the door close behind me with quiet finality.

The walk back to town passes in a blur of rain and tumultuous thoughts. When Mabel's Guesthouse appears through the gray curtain of precipitation, a resolution has formed from emotional chaos.

My laptop awaits where I left it, the article draft glowing on the screen. With newfound clarity, I begin to type—not the exploitative piece Diane requested, but something truer, deeper, about the mountain itself—about respect for wilderness, preparation versus panic, and the thin line between adventure and recklessness.

I write through the evening and into the night, words flowing with unexpected ease. Jackson appears only obliquely—the experienced guide, the voice of caution, the mountain's human guardian. His privacy remains intact while his wisdom permeates every paragraph.

When dawn breaks, the completed draft gleams on my screen—not the career-making exposé Diane wanted, but something I can be proud of. Something that honors both the mountain and the man who protects it.

The submission email feels like cutting the final thread connecting me to Jackson Hart. Three more days in Angel's Peak stretch before me, suddenly interminable without purpose or hope of reconnection.

My phone rings minutes after hitting send, Diane's name flashing insistently on the screen.

"Matthews." Her voice carries excitement rather than the expected disappointment. "You've been holding out on me."

Confusion furrows my brow. "What do you mean?"

"This draft. It's brilliant. The mountain as a character, the respect versus conquest angle. It's exactly what Pathfinder needs right now."

Relief floods through me, unexpected and powerful. "You're not upset about the lack of personal details?"

"Are you kidding? This is better—showing the philosophy without exploiting the man. Makes us look ethical while still getting the substance." Keys clack as she presumably scrolls through the piece. "We want this for the cover. Feature story."

The words I've waited years to hear. My breakthrough moment is finally arriving, yet somehow it feels hollow without someone specific to share it with.

"That's... amazing." The enthusiasm in my voice sounds forced even to my ears.

"There's more." Diane's voice drops conspiratorially. "We want you on staff. Permanent position, travel division. Your own column."

The dream job. Everything I've worked toward. The validation I've craved since journalism school.

"I need to think about it." The words emerge before conscious thought forms.

"Think about it?" Incredulity colors her tone. "Matthews, people kill for this opportunity. What's to think about?"

What indeed? My gaze drifts to the window where mountains rise beyond the town, where a certain cabin sits midway up the slope, where a man who's claimed part of my heart continues his solitary existence.

"Location, mainly." My voice strengthens with each word. "I might have found somewhere new to base myself. For research purposes."

Diane's pause speaks volumes. "You're not talking about Burlington."

"No."

"This wouldn't have anything to do with a certain mountain guide, would it?"

Heat rises to my cheeks despite no one being present to witness it. "It's complicated."

"Always is with the good ones." Her tone softens unexpectedly. "Look, the job's remote-capable. We need you in New York once a month for meetings, but otherwise... The location is flexible."

Hope—dangerous, persistent hope—flutters beneath my ribs. "Really?"

"Don't sound so surprised. It's 2025, Matthews. Welcome to modern journalism." Another pause. "But if you're thinking of staying in Nowheresville for a man, make damn sure he's worth it."

The conversation ends with practical details—salary negotiations, benefit discussions, start dates—but my mind has already leaped to possibilities previously unconsidered.

Outside, the rain has stopped. Sunlight breaks through the dispersing clouds, illuminating mountains still draped in rapidly melting snow. Somewhere up there, Jackson Hart continues his self-imposed isolation, unaware that parameters have shifted, that impossibility has transformed to potential.

The question remains whether he's ready to step beyond the boundaries he's established and whether the connection we forged is strong enough to overcome three years of carefully constructed walls.

Whether, given actual possibility rather than hypothetical longing, he would choose me over the comfortable familiarity of his grief.

Angel's Peak

CHAPTER 11

SUMMIT FEVER

THE MORNING DAWNS CLEAR AND BRIGHT, mountain peaks gleaming against a flawless blue sky. Two days until my departure from Angel's Peak, two days to find closure before returning to a life forever altered by this detour into the wilderness.

My new hiking boots—purchased yesterday from the town's outfitting store—sit by the door, properly broken in after hours of wearing them around my room. Beside them rests a backpack filled with essentials: water, high-protein snacks, first aid kit, emergency blanket, compass, trail map. Everything Jackson taught me during our forced confinement.

Mabel carefully eyes my preparations as I double-check supplies in the guesthouse's cozy kitchen. Her gray hair sits in its usual perfect bun, hands busy kneading dough for the day's bread despite her attention fixed firmly on me.

"You sure about hiking alone, dear? After what happened last time?" She dusts flour from her fingers, worry etched in the creases around her kind eyes.

"I'm prepared this time." The confidence in my voice isn't

feigned. "Weather report's clear, I've got proper gear, and I've logged my route with the ranger station."

Her eyebrows lift at this last detail. "Pete know where you're headed?"

"Lookout Point. Same trail as before." My fingers trace the topographic map spread across the table. "Need to face it, I guess. For closure."

Understanding softens her features. "Some mountains are like that. Need conquering twice—once for survival, once for peace."

The observation surprises me with its insight. "Exactly."

She wraps a homemade energy bar in wax paper, tucking it into my pack. "Jackson know you're going up?"

The question sends an unwelcome pang through my chest. "No. And I'd prefer he didn't."

Not after our last encounter, the memory of which still burns beneath my skin. Not after the silence that followed his gentle rejection. Two days of avoiding town spots where we might intersect, of focusing on interview transcriptions and photo editing rather than impossible hopes.

Mabel's knowing look suggests she understands more than I've shared. "Your secret's safe with me, dear."

The trail looks different in sunlight—less threatening, more inviting. Spring's first tentative efforts brighten the path with tiny wildflowers pushing through melting snow patches. Birds call from awakening trees. Nature in transition, winter reluctantly releasing its grip.

My pace remains deliberately measured, respecting the mountain rather than challenging it. Each step feels like reclaiming something lost—confidence, perhaps, or simple joy in the wilderness without fear shadowing appreciation.

The spot where I slipped on my first disastrous hike appears around a bend, instantly recognizable despite its transformed appearance. Ice has melted, revealing the treacherous rocks that sent me sliding toward near-death. I pause, studying the terrain with new understanding.

Not the mountain's fault. Mine, for rushing, for ignoring warnings, for placing ambition above safety.

The climb continues, muscles warming pleasantly with exertion. My breathing remains controlled despite the elevation, my lungs expanding fully in the crisp mountain air. The familiar burn of physical effort feels cleansing, purifying, washing away lingering regrets with each forward stride.

Approaching the cliff edge where Jackson found me triggers a flood of memories—the rope appearing like magic through blinding snow, his voice cutting through disorientation, strong hands pulling me to safety. The beginning of everything that followed.

The view from the cliff stretches magnificently in all directions—mountain ranges layered to the horizon, valleys etched with silver rivers, forests creating textured carpets of green and white.

Worth the climb.

Worth the risk—the calculated, prepared risk, not the reckless gamble of my first attempt.

Settling on a sun-warmed rock, I extract my notebook and pen from the pack. The article may be finished, submitted, and accepted, but private observations continue to form, demanding expression.

Words flow about perspective gained from elevation, the difference between conquering nature and conversing with it, and mountains as mirrors reflecting human arrogance and resilience.

Time passes unmarked as thoughts transform into sentences on the page. The sun tracks higher, warming my shoulders through the lightweight hiking jacket. Birds soar on thermals below my perch, tiny specks riding invisible currents with effortless grace.

"You came back."

The voice behind me sends my heart lurching against my ribs. I turn slowly, knowing exactly who stands there before visual confirmation arrives.

Jackson Hart—breathtaking against the sky, sunlight catching in his dark hair, expression unreadable behind mirrored sunglasses. His chest rises and falls with slightly elevated breathing, suggesting he climbed quickly after discovering my presence on his mountain.

"Needed to finish what I started." My voice emerges steadier than expected.

He approaches cautiously, stopping several feet away—close enough for conversation, distant enough to avoid accidental contact. "Pete radioed. Said you'd signed the trail log."

Of course. The ranger would naturally inform Jackson of a solo hiker on his mountain, especially one with my history.

"Worried I'd need rescuing again?" The question contains more bite than intended.

Jackson removes his sunglasses, revealing eyes that match the sky's impossible blue. "Concerned. There's a difference."

His gaze shifts to my equipment, assessing with professional attention. Proper boots. Appropriate layers. Well-packed bag. Water bottle within easy reach. Every detail is scrutinized and, judging by his slight nod, approved.

"You've learned." Something like pride colors the observation.

"Had a good teacher." The acknowledgment costs nothing yet feels significant.

He settles on a rock nearby, hands dangling between knees, attention fixed on the panoramic vista rather than me. The silence stretches, not entirely uncomfortable.

"I visited Emma today." The confession emerges unexpectedly, his voice pitched low enough that I almost miss it.

My breath catches, unsure how to respond to this unexpected vulnerability.

"There's a memorial. Near where it happened." His profile remains stoic, controlled. "First time I've gone in months."

"Why today?" The question escapes before wisdom can contain it.

Jackson's jaw works beneath his beard, emotions visibly processed before speech forms. "Needed to talk to her. About things. Changes."

Hope flutters unwelcome in my chest. "What kind of changes?"

"Realizations." His hands clasp together, knuckles whitening momentarily. "That I've been using her memory as an excuse. For hiding. For not living." A deep breath expands his chest. "It's not what she would have wanted."

The admission hangs between us, weightier than the surrounding mountains. My fingers itch to reach for him but remain firmly in my lap, giving space for whatever needs to emerge next.

"You're leaving." Not a question but a statement of fact.

"Day after tomorrow." The reminder sends an unexpected pang through my chest. "Back to Burlington."

Jackson nods once, accepting without visible reaction. "Article finished?"

"Submitted. Accepted." A smile tugs at my lips despite the conversation's heaviness. "Cover feature."

His eyebrows lift slightly. "Congratulations. You earned it."

"Without exploiting you." The clarification feels important. "Your privacy remained intact. I promised."

Something softens around his eyes—gratitude, perhaps respect. "Thank you."

The opening presents itself naturally, heart pounding as

words form. "My editor offered me a staff position. Travel division, my own column."

"That's... impressive." His voice holds genuine warmth. "Everything you wanted, right?"

"Almost everything." The qualifier emerges before caution can censor it. "The interesting part is—it's remote. I'd only need to be in New York monthly for meetings. Could base myself anywhere."

The implication hangs between us, crystal clear yet deliberately unstated. I could stay. If given reason to.

Jackson goes utterly still, processing the revelation with visible intensity. His breathing changes subtly and becomes more controlled. "Anywhere."

"Anywhere with internet access and an airport within reasonable driving distance." My hands busy themselves with notebook pages, needing occupation to mask their slight trembling. "Gives me options I didn't have before."

His throat works as he swallows, his gaze still fixed on distant peaks rather than my face. "Options are good."

The non-committal response drops like a stone in still water. It is not an invitation, not an acknowledgment of possibility, just a bland acceptance of theoretical flexibility.

Disappointment sits heavy in my chest, foolish hope once again crushed beneath reality's weight. What had I expected? For three days of forced proximity and unexpected attraction to overcome three years of grief-imposed isolation?

"Yes, they are." My tone shifts to match his detachment. "Burlington's still the logical choice, though. My apartment, friends, and family are all within driving distance."

Now his eyes finally meet mine, something unreadable flickering in their depths. "Logical."

"Unless there was reason to consider alternatives." The words emerge as a challenge rather than an invitation, pride demanding reciprocal vulnerability.

Jackson's expression shifts—conflict evident in the tightening around his eyes, the slight parting of lips as if words form but remain unspoken. For one breathless moment, possibility hovers between us.

Then his gaze drops, shoulders squaring slightly. "You should choose what makes you happiest, Cloe."

The evasion lands like a physical impact. It's not a rejection, exactly, but the absence of the affirmation needed to justify upending my life. It's not enough.

It's not nearly enough.

"That's the plan." My notebook closes with deliberate finality, sliding into my pack alongside other necessities. "I should head down. Want to catch the afternoon light for some final photos."

Jackson rises with fluid grace, his height momentarily blocking the sun. "I'll walk with you."

Not a request or offer but a statement of fact. The mountain guide asserting professional authority regardless of personal complications.

"Not necessary. I'm fully prepared this time."

"Humor me." His expression brooks no argument. "Consider it my professional obligation."

The descent begins in strained silence, multiple feet of careful distance maintained between us on the narrowing trail. Each step away from the summit feels like a physical representation of opportunity slipping away, of connection breaking with deliberate severing.

Weather shifts subtly as we navigate downward—clouds gathering along distant ridges, temperature dropping incrementally, wind freshening against exposed skin. Nothing threatening, merely nature's constant reminder of its changeable temperament.

"Storm coming tomorrow." Jackson's observation breaks the extended silence. "Good timing for your hike."

"Lucky, I guess." The response emerges flat, emotionally depleted.

More silence follows, punctuated only by boot steps on increasingly muddy trail and distant bird calls. The awkwardness grows with each passing minute, two people with everything and nothing to say occupying the same physical space while emotionally retreating.

At the trail's midpoint, a fallen tree provides a natural resting spot. Jackson pauses, extracting water bottles from his pack, offering one without comment. The gesture feels painfully reminiscent of our shelter days—basic survival courtesies amid deeper currents.

"You're good at this." His voice breaks the silence unexpectedly. "Hiking. Adapting."

The compliment catches me off-guard. "Had proper motivation to learn."

"Beyond survival, I mean." His gaze sweeps across me, professional assessment rather than personal appreciation. "You move differently on the mountain now. With respect. Awareness."

"Again, good teacher." My water bottle suddenly requires intense focus, avoiding eye contact that might reveal too much.

"You'd do well here." The observation emerges casually yet lands with seismic impact. "In these mountains. Given time."

My head snaps up, searching his expression for meaning beyond literal words. "Is that an invitation, Jackson?"

His eyes widen fractionally, caught in unplanned implication. "An observation. Professional assessment."

The clarification extinguishes fragile hope with brutal efficiency. "Right. Professional."

Rising from the log, I shoulder my pack with deliberate independence. "We should continue. Daylight's limited."

The remainder of the descent passes in heavy silence, the

distance between us expanding beyond physical measurement. Each step reinforces what words have confirmed—whatever connection formed in crisis cannot survive in normal life. Whatever he felt wasn't enough to overcome boundaries built from grief and habit.

When the trailhead parking area appears through thinning trees, relief mingles with disappointment. The adventure concludes where it began, a circular journey leading nowhere new.

Jackson pauses as our paths prepare to diverge—his cabin up the service road, town in the opposite direction.

"Will you be at The Pickaxe tonight?" His question emerges stiff, formal. "Locals usually gather for anyone leaving town. Kind of tradition."

The invitation, if it can be called that, holds nothing beyond community courtesy. "Probably not. Packing to do. Early flight."

He nods once, accepting without challenge. "Safe travels then."

Three years of guiding experience, rescue training, wilderness survival expertise—and these inadequate words are all he offers as a goodbye? The mountain man retreating to emotional isolation with the same efficiency he navigated the physical terrain.

His hesitation lasts three heartbeats—I count them against my will, foolishly monitoring for signs of reconsideration. Then he turns, striding toward his waiting truck without a backward glance.

Watching his vehicle disappear around the bend, an unpleasant understanding crystallizes. Some summits remain unconquerable—not because of physical limitations but because the mountain itself refuses approach, prefers isolation to the risk of connection.

Jackson Hart has chosen his path, and it doesn't include

me. My choices narrow accordingly, options collapsing to the single logical direction: forward, away, back to the life temporarily interrupted by mountain misadventure.

The trip back to town stretches longer than physical distance warrants, each step weighted with recognition of what almost was but never would be. The adventure concludes as most adventures must—with a return to ordinary reality, extraordinary possibilities fading to memory with increasing distance.

Two days until departure. Two days to pack belongings and bury unreasonable hopes. Two days to accept that sometimes, even when physically rescued, hearts remain in peril long after their bodies reach safety.

Angel's Peak

Chapter 12

Uncharted Territory

My suitcase lies open on the bed, nearly packed. Clothes folded, toiletries arranged in zippered compartments, hiking boots—still bearing Angel's Peak soil—wrapped in plastic to prevent dirtying other items. Tomorrow morning's flight demands preparation, organization, and finality.

Mabel's homemade scones sit untouched on the bedside table, her concerned hospitality impossible to refuse but equally impossible to consume past the permanent lump in my throat.

Each item placed in the suitcase feels like dismantling the person I've become here, reverting to the Cloe who arrived two weeks ago—ambitious, independent, and utterly unaware of what the mountain wilderness could teach about survival and loss.

A knock at the door interrupts my methodical packing ritual. Probably Mabel with more food I won't eat or questions about my return plans that I can't answer.

The door opens to reveal not Mabel's concerned grandmotherly presence but Jackson Hart—his tall frame filling the doorway, his expression unreadable, his gear pack slung over one powerful shoulder.

Words abandon me completely. He stands perfectly still, seemingly content to let the silence stretch between us. Finally, his throat clears with manufactured casualness.

"Weather window's closing." His eyes meet mine briefly before sliding away. "Last chance to see Mirror Lake before you leave."

The invitation lands like a stone dropped in still water—unexpected, creating ripples of confusion and unwelcome hope.

"Mirror Lake?"

"The place I told you was worth every step." His fingers tighten imperceptibly on the strap crossing his chest. "Four miles round trip, moderate difficulty. Best at sunrise when the mountains reflect perfectly in the water."

"Why?" The question encompasses more than the invitation itself.

Jackson shifts his weight, discomfort evident in the subtle movement. "Thought you might want the experience. For your next article maybe."

Professional justification. Safe, contained, emotionally distant.

"My flight's early tomorrow." The excuse sounds hollow even to my ears.

"Back by sunset." His gaze finally settles directly on mine, something unnamed flickering behind his carefully maintained neutrality. "If you want."

The sensible answer is no. Pack, sleep, and prepare for departure. Don't prolong the inevitable farewell. Don't collect more memories to ache over during sleepless nights in Burlington.

"Let me change." My words escape before wisdom can assert any control.

Twenty minutes later, we're in his truck, climbing the now-familiar mountain road in silence punctuated only by occasional directions as we approach a trailhead I've never visited. The distance between us on the bench seat feels simultaneously too large and not nearly large enough—his presence both comforting and excruciating in its temporary nature.

"Different route than Lookout Point." Jackson's voice breaks the extended silence as he parks at a small clearing where only trail markers indicate human presence. "Less dramatic elevation gain, more diverse terrain."

Professional guide voice. Mountain man dispensing wilderness wisdom. Emotional barriers firmly intact.

The trail begins through a dense pine forest, with dappled sunlight creating intricate patterns across the needle-covered path. Jackson walks slightly ahead, setting a pace considerate of my shorter stride without being condescending. His backpack looks different than yesterday's—larger, containing what appears to be more than emergency supplies for a four-mile hike.

"Why Mirror Lake?" The question emerges as we enter a meadow bursting with early alpine flowers pushing through melting snow patches. "Of all the places to show me on my last day."

Jackson's stride falters momentarily before resuming its steady rhythm. "Told you. Best reflection of the mountains. Worth seeing."

"There are dozens of spots worth seeing in these mountains. You've mentioned several." My persistence surprises us both. "Why this one specifically?"

Several moments pass before he responds, his gaze fixed forward on the trail ahead.

"Personal reasons." The admission emerges reluctantly, each word seemingly extracted with great effort.

We climb in silence after that, the trail winding through

changing ecosystems—dense forest giving way to rocky outcroppings, meadows yielding to streams fed by melting snow. Jackson maintains a steady pace, occasionally pointing out features I'd likely miss without guidance—rare flowers, wildlife tracks pressed into soft mud, rock formations shaped by millennia of harsh weather.

The final ascent steepens considerably, requiring my full attention to navigate the path safely. Jackson's hand appears at particularly challenging sections—offered without comment, withdrawn the moment balance is secured. Each brief contact sends unwelcome electricity through nerve endings that should know better than to respond.

"Almost there." His voice carries quiet anticipation as the trail crests what appears to be a natural ridge.

Then suddenly, breathtakingly—Mirror Lake appears below, a perfect oval of crystal water nestled in a natural bowl of mountain terrain. The lake's surface reflects the surrounding peaks with flawless precision, creating the illusion of mountains growing both upward and downward, meeting at the water's perfect plane.

"Oh." This inadequate syllable escapes on my expelled breath, wholly insufficient against such overwhelming beauty.

Jackson stops beside me, close enough that his arm barely brushes against mine. "Worth it?"

"Beyond words." The truth spills from my lips unbidden.

His smile appears briefly, genuine pleasure at my reaction warming his features momentarily before disappearing behind his typical reserve. "Best spot's this way."

He leads along the lake's perimeter to a natural stone outcropping extending slightly over the water. The view improves with each step, our perspective shifting to capture additional mountain reflections in the lake's still surface.

At the outcropping's end, Jackson removes his pack, extracting what proves to be a small picnic—sandwiches wrapped in wax paper, thermoses of hot coffee, and chocolate chip cookies that look suspiciously like Mabel's recipe.

"You planned this." The observation emerges softer than intended.

Jackson arranges items on a small travel blanket with uncharacteristic care. "Thought you should experience one proper mountain meal before leaving."

The consideration behind this gesture tightens something painful in my chest. Each kindness makes leaving simultaneously harder and more necessary—because kindness isn't enough. Because sandwiches and spectacular views don't equate to genuine wanting, to partnership, to future.

We eat in companionable silence, and the mountains provide a visual feast to accompany our physical sustenance. Birds wheel overhead, their calls echoing across the lake's pristine surface. Occasionally, small fish jump, creating ripples that momentarily distort the perfect reflections before stillness returns.

"I've been coming here since I was six." Jackson's voice breaks the extended silence as he offers unusually personal information without any prompting from me. "My grandfather showed me first. Said it was magic—two worlds meeting at the water line."

Something shifts in his expression—his carefully maintained guard lowering fractionally to reveal the vulnerable man beneath the stoic mountain guide exterior.

"After Emma... this was the only place that still made sense." His fingers tear absently at the grass beside the blanket. "Came here daily for months. Just sitting. Watching the reflections."

My breath catches at this unexpected vulnerability. "Why show me?"

His gaze remains fixed on distant mountains rather than my face. "Wanted you to see it. Before leaving."

Not the complete answer, but perhaps all he's capable of offering. The unspoken hovers between us—regret, possibility, roads untaken.

Time passes differently in this pristine setting, measured by shifting light across mountain faces and the subtle lengthening of shadows as afternoon progresses toward evening. Conversation ebbs and flows naturally, touching on safe topics —my article details his upcoming guide season, memories of our shelter confinement carefully edited to exclude emotional entanglements.

"We should start back soon." Jackson's observation coincides with the sun dipping toward western peaks. "Want to reach the trailhead before dusk."

Reality intrudes with his practical words—this interlude ending, departure approaching with every passing minute. The knowledge settles like a physical weight, making movements leaden as we pack the remaining picnic items.

At the outcropping's edge, Jackson pauses, his gaze sweeping across the panoramic view with unusual intensity, as if committing details to memory.

"I've never brought anyone here before." His admission emerges quietly from his lips, almost imperceptibly in the mountain stillness. "Not since Emma."

The revelation sends unexpected warmth through my chest despite everything. "Why me?"

His profile remains stoic against the darkening sky, his jaw working slightly beneath his beard. Seconds stretch to nearly a minute before he responds.

"Needed you to understand something about me." The words emerge with evident difficulty. "Before you left."

"Understand what?" Hope flutters traitorously beneath my ribs.

Jackson finally turns, his eyes meeting mine with uncharacteristic directness. Something powerful lurks in the blue depths of his eyes—conflict, perhaps pain, something far beyond the careful neutrality he typically maintains.

"That I'm trying." His voice roughens slightly. "It's just..."

The sentence hangs unfinished, those two words encompassing volumes of unspoken meaning. He's trying—to move beyond grief, to connect, to imagine possibility beyond isolation? Trying but not succeeding.

Not enough, anyway.

Words gather in my throat—encouragements, reassurances, declarations—but pride contains them. I've already revealed enough and offered enough openings. The next move must be his, fully and completely.

"I understand." My response emerges gently from my throat despite the disappointment crushing beneath my sternum like a physical weight.

His hand lifts slightly, as if reaching for me, before dropping back to his side. Another almost. Another not quite. Another moment where capability fails to manifest as action.

The descent begins in silence, heavier than before, weighted with knowledge of what won't be said and what won't be done. Each step away from Mirror Lake feels symbolic—retreating from beauty, from possibility, from the man walking slightly ahead who cannot quite reach for what he almost wants.

Midway down, Jackson pauses unexpectedly at a viewpoint overlooking the valley beyond. The sun hangs low, casting golden light across the landscape transformed by approaching evening. His profile in this illumination appears almost sculpted—strong jaw, straight nose, eyes reflecting amber tones rather than their usual blue.

"Cloe." My name emerges with unusual softness. "I—"

Hope rises unwelcome and powerful. My breath halts, waiting for words that might change everything.

"I hope you find what you're looking for." The sentence

completes with devastating finality. "In Burlington. With your writing. Everything."

Not what I hoped for. Not even close.

"Thank you, and thank you for today." My voice emerges surprisingly steady. "For showing me this place."

His nod acknowledges without requiring further speech. The moment passes between us, this fleeting opportunity evaporating like morning dew under the rising sun.

We continue downward along the trail, our conversation limited to necessary observations and his occasional warnings about loose rocks or slippery sections. We maintain professional courtesy despite the emotional undercurrents flowing between us.

The trailhead appears as dusk settles across the landscape, the final light of the day painting the mountains in purple and gold. Jackson's truck waits where we left it, a symbol of our impending separation more final than physical distance.

The drive to town passes largely in silence, punctuated only by necessary conversation about my flight details, transportation arrangements, and final packing needs. Surface-level exchange masking depths neither of us seems willing to acknowledge directly.

Outside Mabel's Guesthouse, Jackson shifts the truck into park, but leaves the engine running—a clear signal that extended goodbyes aren't planned. His hands remain on the steering wheel, knuckles whitening slightly with pressure.

"Thank you." The words encompass everything and nothing—for rescue, for shelter, for Mirror Lake, for showing me parts of himself even while withholding what matters most. "For everything."

Jackson nods once, gaze fixed forward through the windshield rather than meeting mine. "Safe travels tomorrow."

His dismissal lands with a finality that steals my breath, leaving me frozen. This is it. The end.

No dramatic declarations, no last-minute changes of heart. Just a practical farewell from a man who cannot, will not step beyond boundaries constructed from grief and habit.

My hand reaches for the door handle, pride straightening my spine despite the hollow ache spreading beneath my ribs. "Goodbye, Jackson."

Something shifts in his expression—conflict evident in the tightening around his eyes and the slight parting of his lips, as if words form but remain trapped. His hand moves suddenly, catching mine before I can exit the vehicle.

"Cloe." My name emerges rough-edged, almost desperate.

Then his mouth finds mine, the kiss containing everything his words cannot express—longing, regret, desire, farewell. His hand cradles my face with heartbreaking gentleness that contrasts with the almost desperate pressure of his lips.

For several suspended moments, hope resurges within me—perhaps this physical declaration precedes verbal commitment. Perhaps touch communicates what speech cannot formulate.

When we finally separate, our breathing ragged and uneven, his expression reveals raw emotion that he typically conceals behind his careful control. His vulnerability lies fully exposed, his defenses momentarily lowered in this rare unguarded moment.

"I can't—" His words emerge strained, pained. "I'm not—"

Not ready. Not healed enough. Not capable of offering what I deserve.

"I know." My acceptance costs me everything but allows me to maintain my dignity intact. "It's okay."

It's not okay. Nothing about this situation approaches okay. But pretending otherwise serves no purpose beyond prolonging inevitable pain.

His forehead rests briefly against mine, our shared breath

creating an intimacy beyond physical connection. Then he pulls away, walls visibly rebuilding with each passing second.

"Goodbye, Cloe Matthews." The words carry finality impossible to misinterpret.

The guesthouse door closes behind me with quiet decisiveness. Through the window, Jackson's truck remains idling for several heartbeats before finally pulling away, taillights disappearing around the corner like dying embers.

Mabel appears in the hallway, concern evident in her lined face. "Everything alright, dear?"

"Fine." The lie emerges with surprising steadiness. "Just finished packing. All set for tomorrow."

She nods without believing, her kindness preventing further questioning. "There's tea if you'd like some. Might help you sleep before your flight."

Sleep seems entirely implausible, but the gesture deserves acknowledgment. "Thank you. Maybe later."

My room welcomes me with its impersonal comfort—all traces of temporary occupancy erased, belongings contained in luggage ready for departure. The space could belong to anyone or no one. My presence here is already fading like footprints in fresh snow.

Morning arrives after a night of restless half-sleep, dreams filled with mountain paths leading nowhere and blue eyes full of things left unspoken. Angel's Peak recedes through the rear window as I drive to the small regional airport. The mountains stubbornly maintain their eternal presence regardless of the human dramas enacted in their shadow.

I turn in my rental car and hop on the airport shuttle. The driver loads my luggage while chatting about expected clear flying conditions.

The airport appears with disappointing swiftness—a small regional facility with direct connections to Denver, where larger planes will carry me eventually back to Burlington.

Check-in, security, waiting area—I move mechanically through each step of these processes, which require minimal conscious thought from me. Other passengers blur into the background noise as I stare through large windows at mountains still visible in the distance.

The boarding call comes too soon and not soon enough. The final passengers file onto the small regional jet, and flight attendants perform routine safety demonstrations. The engines rumble to life beneath the floor, vibrations traveling through the seat into bones still aching from different, deeper tremors.

As the plane taxis toward the runway, my gaze fixes on the terminal building's observation deck. A solitary figure stands at the railing—tall, broad-shouldered, unmistakable even at this distance.

Jackson.

He came to watch my departure. Not to stop it, not to change it, simply to witness. He came to witness the final act of our brief, intense connection as it concludes with a physical separation that mirrors the emotional distance he has already established between us.

The plane accelerates down the runway, its wheels lifting from the tarmac as we take flight. Through the window, his figure diminishes until its indistinguishable from the building, then the landscape, then lost entirely as clouds envelop the climbing aircraft.

When the seatbelt sign extinguishes, I extract my laptop and notebook from the carry-on stowed beneath the seat. Professional habits provide comfort in their familiarity— document open, cursor blinking, words waiting to be captured and arranged.

But instead of notes for upcoming articles or edits to existing work, my fingers hover briefly before typing an unexpected heading:

THE MOUNTAIN BETWEEN US

Not a magazine piece. Not travel journalism. Something else entirely—a story about a writer and a mountain man. About rescue and risk, wounds too deep for casual healing and connections too strong to dismiss.

Unlike reality's messy, unfinished conclusion, this story will find a happy ending. The fictional mountain man will overcome his fears. The writer will find her courage. Their paths will converge rather than diverge.

The words flow with surprising ease. Outside the small oval window, clouds part to reveal a landscape that grows increasingly unfamiliar, trading the wilderness for the bustle of humanity.

Burlington awaits with comfortable familiarity—my apartment, friends, career advancement, life interrupted but now resuming. The future stretches with promise and possibility.

Yet as the plane continues its journey away from Angel's Peak, something remains behind—not just memories or experiences, but pieces of myself transformed by the crisp mountain air, unforgiving terrain, and a man who taught survival in more ways than he intended.

Some rescues, it seems, remain permanently incomplete and forever unfinished.

Angel's Peak

Chapter 13

Whiteout

The applause feels hollow, echoing across the sleek conference room as Editor-in-Chief Vivian Mercer holds up the latest issue of *Venture* magazine. My feature article on Angel's Peak dominates the cover—a breathtaking panorama captured during that golden sunset on my last evening there. My name sprawls across the bottom in elegant serif font: *Cloe Bennett*.

"This, people, is how you write a travel piece." Vivian taps her manicured nail against my byline. "Authentic. Immersive. Without turning into some invasive exposé on the locals."

Her praise should warm me. Instead, the air conditioning chills my skin despite the April sunshine streaming through floor-to-ceiling windows. The Manhattan skyline stretches beyond the glass—jagged, magnificent, utterly foreign after six weeks back in the city.

My colleagues nod appreciatively, several offering congratulatory smiles. I return them automatically, muscle memory taking over where genuine emotion fails. The article has already generated record engagement metrics, subscription bumps, and industry buzz. By every professional measure, it's the pinnacle of success.

So why does it feel like I'm standing at the bottom of a mountain I no longer want to climb?

"Shall we break for lunch? Cloe, my office at two." Vivian dismisses the editorial team with her typical brisk efficiency.

I gather my notebook, running fingers across the embossed leather cover—a gift to myself after my first major byline three years ago. Back when every achievement felt significant, every editor's nod validating. Before a mountain guide with storm-gray eyes and calloused hands showed me what it meant to genuinely connect with a place.

With a person.

A person unwilling to fight to keep me.

Jackson's face materializes in my mind, unbidden but never unwelcome. The stern line of his jaw softening as he finally allowed himself to laugh. The reverent way his fingers traced ridgelines on maps. The vulnerability in his voice when he finally spoke of Emma.

"You've been somewhere else for weeks."

I startle at Vivian's voice. She leans against the doorframe, arms crossed, observing me with the same penetrating gaze that's made her legendary in publishing circles. At forty-five, she embodies metropolitan success—tailored charcoal pantsuit, sleek silver bob, posture suggesting both authority and ease in wielding it.

"Just distracted by the Bainbridge assignment," I lie.

"Bullshit." Vivian steps fully into the room, closing the door behind her. "Your work is impeccable as always. But you're here—" she taps her temple, "—about sixty percent of the time. The rest of you never came back from Colorado."

My cheeks burn. Vivian has always possessed an unnerving ability to see through professional facades. It's what makes her both an exceptional editor and a terrifying boss.

"The Angel's Peak piece is your best work. Know why?" She doesn't wait for my response. "Because you actually gave a damn. You weren't just observing life—you were living it."

The truth in her assessment stings.

"The Simpson feature next week, then the magazine celebration at The Atrium. After that..." She scrutinizes me over sleek reading glasses. "Maybe we discuss some adjustments to your arrangement here."

Ice water floods my veins. "Are you firing me?"

Vivian's laugh is genuine, if short. "Quite the opposite. I'm trying to keep the best writer I've ever hired from sleepwalking through a career she's outgrown." She moves toward the door. "Wear something spectacular tomorrow night. The Atrium event is bringing every publishing heavyweight in the city."

She pauses at the threshold. "Oh, and Cloe? Whatever's holding your attention in Colorado? Might be worth examining why it's got such a grip."

The Atrium glitters with Manhattan opulence—a glass-domed sanctuary twenty floors above Columbus Circle, where crystal chandeliers refract light across white marble floors and verdant living walls. String quartet music weaves through the murmur of industry conversations. Champagne flows freely, paired with canapés crafted by some Michelin-starred chef whose name is highlighted in the invitation.

I adjust the neckline of my dress—midnight blue silk that cost more than I'm willing to admit—and plaster on my networking smile. Fashion editor Renata Marks approaches, trailing a cloud of exotic perfume.

"Darling, absolute triumph with the mountain piece." She air-kisses near both my cheeks. "Though honestly, who knew there was anything worth experiencing in some obscure Colorado town? Did you have to sleep in an actual cabin?"

My fingers tighten around the champagne flute. "Angel's Peak has unexpected depth."

"Well, it translated beautifully. Though I can't imagine spending more than the absolute required time there." She shivers theatrically. "No proper restaurants? No boutiques? What did you even do?"

Learn to navigate whiteout conditions.

Watch sunlight transform mountainsides into cathedrals.

Feel truly alive for perhaps the first time in my life.

"Research," I reply instead, taking another sip of champagne that no longer satisfies. The vintage Krug leaves nothing but bitterness on my tongue now.

Across the room, Vivian holds court with several publishing executives. She catches my eye, subtly tilting her head toward them—a clear invitation to join the career-advancing conversation.

Three months ago, I would have immediately gravitated to that circle, armed with carefully rehearsed insights and strategic questions. Now, I find myself moving toward the floor-to-ceiling windows instead, seeking the comfort of the open sky.

The city sprawls below in all its electric glory—a constellation of human ambition and ingenuity stretched across the darkness. Beautiful in its way, yet utterly different from the star-strewn sky above Angel's Peak. Here, even the brightest stars are rendered invisible by the city's relentless illumination.

Just like pieces of myself have become invisible amid professional aspirations.

"Ms. Bennett?"

I turn toward the unfamiliar voice—a young attendant in crisp black attire.

"Someone's asking for you at reception. Says it's important."

Curiosity pulls me from my window refuge. Perhaps a latecomer from the West Coast bureau? Or another editor hoping to poach me, as occasionally happens at these functions?

The elevator bank sits removed from the main celebration, soft lighting replacing the brilliant display of the main hall. I round the corner and stop dead.

Jackson Hart stands by the reception desk.

My heart performs a complex acrobatic sequence in my chest. He's wearing dark jeans and a charcoal button-down—clearly his version of formal attire—with his hair actually combed, though one rebellious wave falls across his forehead and curls above his brow. He looks simultaneously uncomfortable and determined, shifting his weight in shoes that appear suspiciously new.

"Jackson?" His name escapes in a whisper.

He turns, his expression transforming from uncertainty to something akin to relief.

"Cloe."

Just my name, in that low, slightly rough voice that's haunted my dreams for six weeks. He takes a half step forward, then stops, suddenly seeming aware of our surroundings—the sleek modern lobby with its abstract art and uniformed staff.

"What are you doing in New York?" The question emerges more breathlessly than intended.

"Reading." His lips quirk in that almost-smile that I've missed with embarrassing intensity. From his jacket pocket, he produces a folded copy of *Venture* magazine. "You made the mountain sound beautiful."

"It is beautiful."

"Not the way most city people see it."

We stand in suspended animation, three feet apart yet separated by worlds. Behind me, string music and cultivated laughter filter from the celebration. Before me stands a man who belongs to granite peaks and pine forests, looking as out of place in this chrome and glass environment as a wolf in a perfumery.

Shadows linger beneath his eyes, suggesting troubled sleep. The familiar scar across his left knuckles stands out against tanned skin, but something in his posture has shifted—a subtle easing of the rigid guard he maintained on the mountain.

"You didn't mention Emma in the article." He says this quietly, gratitude evident in his tone.

"It wasn't my story to tell."

His eyes hold mine, storm-gray intensity that sees beyond practiced social veneers. "But you told all the other stories perfectly. The mountain after fresh snow. The way light changes the north face at sunset. That ridiculous coffee shop where Mabel threatens customers who request almond milk."

A startled laugh escapes me. "She nearly banished me when I asked for soy."

"She references 'that city girl journalist' at least twice weekly." His expression softens. "The town misses you."

The unspoken question lingers between us—does he?

Jackson shifts, reaching into his jacket again. This time he withdraws a small object, cradling it momentarily before extending his hand toward me.

A compass rests in his palm—vintage brass with a weathered leather case, clearly well-used but meticulously maintained.

"Emma's," he says, answering my unasked question. "It's saved my life more times than I can count."

The significance of this offering steals my breath. I make no move to take it, understanding the magnitude of what he's sharing.

"There was an accident on the north face three weeks ago." His voice remains steady, but tension threads through his posture. "Family of four. Intermediate hikers who ignored weather warnings. Got caught in a sudden spring storm."

My journalist's instincts prickle. "The Sandovals? I saw something online—"

"All four made it down alive." His jaw tightens. "But only because someone went up after them."

Understanding dawns slowly. "You led a rescue. The exact kind of rescue—"

"That killed Emma. Yes." His eyes meet mine unflinchingly. "I've spent years avoiding those calls, letting others take the high-risk rescues. Telling myself it was because they were better qualified."

"But really, it was fear," I finish softly.

"Turns out I was more afraid of living half a life than facing that mountain again." Something vulnerable crosses his expression. "Your article arrived the day before the call came in. Reading how you saw Angel's Peak—how you saw potential where I only saw pain—it shifted something inside of me."

He extends the compass again, this time with gentle insistence. "Emma would want you to have this. She believed tools should go to people who'd use them to explore, not those who'd lock them away as memorials."

My fingers brush his as I accept the compass. Its weight feels significant beyond its physical presence—a talisman of both past tragedy and future possibility.

"Jackson, I don't understand why you're here."

"That storm on the mountain?" He gestures vaguely upward as though the snow-capped peaks of Colorado might be visible through Manhattan's light pollution. "You called it a whiteout in your article. Said it was terrifying and beautiful at once—how everything familiar disappeared, forcing you to navigate by other means."

I nod, remembering the disorienting swirl of white, the way Jackson became my only reference point.

"I've been living in a different kind of whiteout since Emma died." His voice drops, meant only for me despite the empty lobby. "Using grief as an excuse to stop moving forward. Reading your words, I realized I've been deliberately staying lost."

He steps closer, the subtle scent of pine and mountain air somehow still clinging to him despite the city surroundings.

"The day after the rescue..." His voice scrapes raw, words dragged from somewhere deep. "I hiked to Emma's favorite summit." He looks up, eyes shadowed with memory and something fiercer—something new. "First time since she died. I told her about you."

A string quartet surges in the distance, each note winding through the cold Manhattan air like a thread pulling me toward him. The music crescendos—sharp, aching—as if the whole world knows what he's about to say.

"I can't keep living between what was and what might be." His hands flex at his sides. Not shaking. But close. Those hands that pulled me out of the storm and held me through the night. Calloused. Steady. Honest.

"I guide summer expeditions on Angel's Peak. But winters..." His voice dips, low and rough, eyes never leaving mine. "I could base winters wherever your work takes you. Manhattan, if needed."

A pause. Not hesitation—just breath. Just the beat before everything changes.

"I should've asked you to stay." His voice is hoarse with the weight of regret. "You certainly gave me enough opportunity to ask. I realize that now. I've thought about it every damn day since I let you walk out of my life."

His eyes lock on mine, unflinching. "I want to be with you. I need to be part of your life."

Each word hits like a heartbeat—steady, deliberate, devastating.

"Whatever it takes. Whatever it costs." He takes a slow step closer, like he's afraid he's already lost me. "I'm in."

The words hang between us, weighted with everything he's never said. His jaw tightens, and for the first time, his eyes flicker—not with resolve, but with fear. The kind that lives deep in the bones. The kind that only comes when you care too much.

"But only if..." His voice breaks slightly, barely audible over the pulse roaring in my ears. "Only if you still want me. If I haven't already wrecked this beyond repair."

His shoulders go still. Braced for the blow.

Not because he doesn't mean every word.

But because he's terrified it might be too late to say them.

It couldn't be more perfectly Jackson Hart.

No grand gesture. No fanfare.

Just a man, standing in the middle of a city he doesn't belong to, offering his heart like it's the only thing he has left —and the only thing that matters.

A laugh escapes me—sharp, stunned, soaked in disbelief, and something dangerously close to joy.

Jackson's brow furrows. His jaw tightens. That flicker of uncertainty flashes in his eyes, like he's bracing for rejection. Again.

I take a breath, pulse skittering. "I shouldn't have walked away."

His gaze snaps to mine.

"I gave you every chance to ask me to stay, but I should've stayed anyway. I told myself I was giving you space, letting you go with dignity." My throat thickens. "But the truth is, I left my heart in Angel's Peak. And the minute I got back here, I started figuring out how to get it back."

His expression shifts—hope warring with disbelief.

"Yesterday, I submitted a proposal to Vivian—my editor at the magazine," I add, stepping closer. "Remote work. Based in

Angel's Peak. Travel for major assignments. Quarterly office visits."

His breath stutters. "You—"

"It's already approved. I start next month." The words settle between us, anchoring something that had been weightless and uncertain for too long. "I tried convincing myself I belonged here. That Angel's Peak was just another story. But—"

"The mountain gets in your blood," he says.

"No." I shake my head, locking eyes with him. "*You* did."

He exhales like I just punched the air back into his lungs.

Then he moves.

One step. Two. And I'm in his arms, hauled against his chest with a force that steals my breath.

His mouth crashes down on mine—hot, hungry, claiming.

The kiss isn't gentle. It's weeks of want. Of regret. Of everything we didn't say. His hands grip my waist, fingers digging in like he's making sure I'm real.

I kiss him back just as hard.

Around us, the gala swirls—clinking glasses, muted laughter, a string quartet playing something delicate and expensive.

But I only feel him—solid and steady and finally mine.

Angel's Peak

Chapter 14

Epilogue

Home Base

The late afternoon sunlight filters through pine boughs, casting dappled shadows across the newly stained deck. One year to the day since I officially moved to Angel's Peak, and the cabin—our cabin—finally feels complete. The renovations took months: expanding the kitchen, adding the writer's nook with windows overlooking the valley, reinforcing the foundation to withstand even the harshest winter storms.

Just like our relationship.

"You're getting philosophical again." Jackson emerges from the cabin carrying two steaming mugs. His hair is longer now, sun-streaked from a summer of guiding, curling slightly against the nape of his neck. He's relaxed in a way I never witnessed during those first tension-filled days on the mountain—ease in his movements, smile lines deepening around his eyes.

"How could you possibly know what I'm thinking?" I accept the coffee, breathing in the rich aroma that chases away the October chill.

"That's your writer face." He settles beside me on the porch swing we installed last month, his thigh warm against mine. "Contemplative. Slightly smug. Usually means you're crafting some profound metaphor about mountains and relationships."

Heat rises to my cheeks. "I hate that you know me so well."

"Liar." His arm slides around my shoulders, drawing me closer.

Beyond our clearing, Angel's Peak rises majestic against the cloudless sky. The same mountain that nearly killed me now grounds me—its moods and seasons marking the rhythm of our life together. Summer brought Jackson's expanded guide business, including the wildly popular photography tours inspired by my *Venture* spreads. Fall has delivered crisp mornings and the kind of golden light photographers dream about.

And my book.

The one I started scribbling on the plane, over frozen peaks and broken goodbyes, was my attempt to rewrite the ending of my story with Jackson. A love story with a happily ever after rather than broken hearts and tears.

What began as scattered notes during a blizzard became something more intimate than anything I'd ever published.

A love story.

Not the one I lived, but the one I wished I had.

A rewrite of the ending I couldn't bear to accept.

It wasn't meant for anyone to read. Just a way to bleed it out—quietly, safely—onto the page.

Now it's a bestseller. Hitting every list. A sweeping tale of fiction for readers who'll never know what really happened in that storm.

"Nervous about tonight?" Jackson's question vibrates through his chest, where my head now rests.

"Terrified." I trace the rim of my mug. "It's one thing to

have the book released nationally. It's another to face everyone in town who can separate fact from fiction."

His chuckle rumbles beneath my ear. "They've been speculating about us since your first visit. This just gives them new material."

"Mabel already asked if the scene on page 127 really happened."

Jackson nearly chokes on his coffee. "Please tell me you didn't answer."

"I just smiled mysteriously and ordered more pie."

That particular scene—one of several intimate moments in the book transformed through the lens of fiction—still makes me blush when I consider how closely it mirrors reality. The night after that first successful rescue, when Jackson finally allowed himself to fully open up about Emma, about fear, about second chances. The way gentle conversation transformed into something hungrier, healing.

"I still can't believe your editor didn't make you change more details." Jackson's fingers idly stroke my shoulder, a gesture so familiar now it's become as essential as breathing.

"Vivian knows when truth serves the story better than invention." My gaze drifts to the small shrine we've created on the bookshelves inside—Emma's compass flanked by first-edition copies of *The Mountain Between Us*. "Besides, some details are changed. Names. Timeline."

"Not enough to fool anyone in Angel's Peak."

"No," I agree. "But enough to make it technically fiction."

The advance copies scattered around town have already sparked debate at Mabel's Diner, the general store, and the seasonal festivals that mark small-town life.

How much is real? Which parts are embellished? Did they really get trapped together during that blizzard, or was that artistic license?

The speculation amuses more than it bothers. This community has become family in ways Manhattan never managed despite my decade there. Here, neighbors bring casseroles when someone's sick. They shovel each other's driveways after heavy snowfall. They show up—physically, emotionally, consistently.

Jackson checks his watch—a gift from the Sandoval family after the rescue, engraved with a simple *Thank You*. "We should probably head down soon. Mabel threatened bodily harm if we're late to your book celebration."

"Five more minutes," I murmur, not ready to share this moment with anyone else.

Jackson kisses the top of my head, understanding without words. We've developed this language over months of learning each other—when to push, when to yield, when to simply sit in companionable silence as the mountain changes colors around us.

The renovation of the high-altitude emergency shelter last spring became a metaphor for our relationship—reinforcing foundations, expanding comfort without sacrificing function, preserving what worked while improving what didn't. The old cabin where we sheltered during the blizzard has transformed into a proper waystation, complete with communication equipment, expanded supplies, and detailed maps of escape routes.

"Did I tell you Pete's adding a special display of your book at the general store?" Jackson's voice draws me back to the present. "Right next to the tourist souvenirs. Says he's going to market Angel's Peak as a literary destination now."

I groan. "Next, they'll be offering walking tours of locations from the book."

"Already happening. Joline at the visitor center has a handwritten map for dedicated readers." His smile crinkles the corners of his eyes. "The trail to the north face overlook has never seen so much traffic."

"You're enjoying this far too much."

"Watching my fiercely private girlfriend navigate small-town celebrity? Absolutely." He shifts, reaching into his pocket. "Which reminds me. Something to commemorate publication day."

The small box he produces isn't wrapped, just tied with a simple leather cord that looks hand-braided. My heart stutters with an emotion too complex to name.

"Jackson..."

"Open it before you panic." His expression holds gentle amusement. "It's not a ring. At least, not yet."

The qualifier sends warmth cascading through me.

He shifts just enough that our knees brush. "That's coming. When the timing's right. When I can do it the way I want—on one knee, under the open sky, probably somewhere that smells like pine and snow."

His thumb grazes mine, slow and sure. "But this... this is me saying I'm not going anywhere."

We've discussed marriage—a someday possibility rather than an immediate plan—but the casual way he references it now speaks volumes about how far we've traveled from those first guarded interactions.

Inside the box rests a pendant on a delicate silver chain. The pendant itself is circular, crafted from brushed silver with what appears to be a topographical map etched into its surface. Tiny gemstones mark two specific locations.

"The blue sapphire marks where I found you in the storm." Jackson's voice softens. "The diamond marks the cabin. Where you found me."

I trace the intricate lines with my fingertip, recognizing the familiar contours of Angel's Peak rendered in precious metal.

The craftsmanship is extraordinary—each ridge and valley is meticulously detailed.

"Marianne in town helped design it, but I had it made by a silversmith in Denver." His eyes search mine. "Do you like it?"

Words fail. Instead, I turn, lifting my hair so he can fasten the necklace. The pendant rests perfectly in the hollow of my throat, cool against my skin but quickly warming.

"It's the most meaningful gift I've ever received."

When I turn back, his expression has shifted—intensity replacing relaxed affection. His hand rises to cup my cheek, thumb brushing the corner of my mouth with deliberate tenderness.

"I never imagined this life was possible." The confession emerges roughly. "After Emma, I convinced myself that kind of connection was a once-in-a-lifetime occurrence."

"And now?" My fingers find his wrist, feeling his pulse quicken beneath my touch.

"Now I know better." His forehead rests against mine. "Some connections aren't about replacing what was lost. They're about creating something entirely new."

The kiss starts slow.

A brush of lips. Soft. Seeking.

Jackson's never been good at slow with me—not when the stakes are real. And right now, every breath between us feels like a fuse burning low.

His hand slides into my hair, mouth slanting over mine with more pressure, more urgency. My dress shifts against his sweater, my fingers digging beneath the hem to touch the skin I already know by heart.

He groans—deep and rough—and then we're moving.

He stands, lifting me without warning. My legs wrap around his waist, arms locking around his shoulders as the swing creaks behind us, swaying empty in the chill mountain air.

His boots thud heavy across the porch, then the threshold, as the cabin door slams shut behind us with a sharp finality. He doesn't hesitate. Doesn't fumble. Just slams me back against the wall with enough force to knock the air from my lungs and my soul straight into my throat.

His mouth finds mine again—hard, claiming, breath like fire.

My hands fumble between us, tugging at the waistband of his jeans. He doesn't wait. One hand braces me against the wall, the other yanks down his zipper with a rough, impatient sound. The heat of him presses against me, thick and ready.

He shoves my dress up with both hands, baring me in seconds, fingers dragging over slick skin.

He thrusts into me in one brutal, perfect stroke, and my body arches like it's trying to take all of him.

"*Fuuuuck*, Cloe..." His voice breaks over my name. "I'll never get enough of this. Of you."

I cry out—choked, desperate—fingers scrabbling against his shoulders, needing something to hold while he drives into me, again and again, hard enough to rattle the pictures on the wall.

"Look at me," he growls, breath hot against my neck. "Want to see your face when you come."

I do. Eyes locked on his. Skin flushed. Mouth open. Every thrust deeper, rougher, dragging pleasure from somewhere sharp and aching and holy.

"Jackson—"

"I've got you," he pants. "I've always got you."

My release hits like a detonation—white-hot and blinding. My body clenches around him as I cry out, nails digging into his back. He follows with a ragged groan, hips slamming into mine one last time before he shudders, buried deep.

We collapse against the wall, breath ragged, bodies still trembling.

His forehead presses to mine, our skin damp, the air between us pulsing with heat and satisfaction.

The pendant swings between us, catching the light as it rests against his chest—between heartbeats that finally begin to slow.

He kisses my temple. Then, my jaw. Then, the corner of my mouth.

"Now we're going to be late," he murmurs, voice wrecked with satisfaction.

I smirk, tugging my dress down without the slightest apology. "Worth it."

He chuckles low, his hands still possessive on my hips.

"Mabel's going to take one look at us and know exactly what happened."

"Good." His grin is wicked.

The sun hangs low as we finally descend toward town, Jackson's truck navigating the familiar switchbacks with practiced ease. His hand rests on my knee, thumb tracing absent circles as Angel's Peak watches over our journey from above.

"Think you'll ever miss New York?" The question comes casually, but I catch the underlying current of vulnerability.

"I miss specific things. Good Thai food delivery at midnight. Art galleries on rainy afternoons." I cover his hand with mine. "But I don't miss my life there."

His smile reaches his eyes, and the crow's feet deepen. "That shelter renovation project is wrapping up next month. I was thinking we might take a trip after. Your choice of destination."

"Hmm. Somewhere with unreliable cell service and limited internet?"

"Naturally." His grin turns mischievous. "Though I suppose we could consider a city. Museums. Theater. All those cultured activities you claim to miss."

The teasing is familiar—his pretend reluctance about

urban adventures balanced against my feigned complaints about wilderness expeditions. The truth lies somewhere between: we've found balance in alternating environments, collecting experiences rather than compromising passions.

Mabel's Diner comes into view, windows glowing warm gold against encroaching twilight. Congratulatory banners are strung all across its facade. Mabel's Diner overflows with familiar faces, all gathered to celebrate not just my book but the story we've all created together—a story of community, second chances, and mountains, both literal and metaphorical.

"Ready?" Jackson squeezes my hand as he parks.

I touch the map pendant at my throat, feeling its weight like an anchor connecting me to both what was and what will be. The coordinates of past and present, marked in precious metal against my skin.

"Ready."

As we step from the truck, the diner door bursts open, spilling golden light and welcoming voices into the mountain evening. Hands reach for us, drawing us into the warmth of celebration. Questions and congratulations tumble over each other. Mabel makes pointed comments about our tardiness, which has several townspeople snickering knowingly.

Through it all, Jackson's hand stays firm against the small of my back—steady, grounding, a silent promise that wherever I go, he's with me. Like a compass, like a tether. Like home.

Some paths, I once thought I had to walk alone, but the greatest climbs—the ones that break you open and build you back stronger—those are never meant to be faced alone. Those are meant to be climbed together.

And far above us, dusted in snow and golden light, Angel's Peak rises against the sky—a silent witness and eternal sentinel —watching over us as we begin the next ascent.

Together.

LOVE THE HEAT, DANGER, AND HEART IN ANGEL'S Peak?

Get ready to hike higher, fall harder, and surrender deeper...

Up next: Stranded with the Resort Owner

When perfectionist event coordinator Amelia Hayes arrives at The Haven at Angel's Peak, she's ready to execute the high-profile wedding that could launch her career—until a blizzard traps her alone with the resort's infuriatingly attractive owner.

Lucas Cross left his cutthroat corporate past behind to restore his family's mountain resort. The last thing he needs is a control-freak planner storming into his quiet sanctuary... or the undeniable attraction that ignites the moment they crash into each other—literally—on the icy steps.

With the wedding staff snowed out and the power down, Amelia and Lucas are forced to share his remote cabin—complete with one bed, no backup, and a rising heat that has nothing to do with the fire. As their forced proximity turns to something deeper, they'll have to confront what matters more: keeping control... or letting love in.

But when the snow clears and real life closes in, will their connection melt away—or spark something permanent?

TROPES YOU'LL LOVE:

- Forced Proximity
- One Bed
- Grumpy/Sunshine
- Opposites Attract
- Workaholic Heroine
- Reclusive, Protective Hero

- Dominant Dirty Talk
- High-Stakes Career vs. Love

DON'T MISS WHAT HAPPENS NEXT IN ANGEL'S Peak—where passion is raw, the mountains are unforgiving, and love comes when you least expect it.

Read: Stranded with the Resort Owner today.

Angel's Peak

Please consider leaving a review

I hope you enjoyed this book as much as I enjoyed writing it. If you like this book, please leave a review. I love reviews. I love reading your reviews, and they help other readers decide if this book is worth their time and money. I hope you think it is and decide to share this story with others. A sentence is all it takes. Thank you in advance!

Click on the link below to leave your review
Goodreads
Amazon
Bookbub

Angel's Peak

ELLZ BELLZ

Ellie's Facebook Reader Group

If you are interested in joining the ELLZ BELLZ, Ellie's
Facebook reader group, we'd love to have you.

Join Ellie's ELLZ BELLZ.
The ELLZ BELLZ Facebook Reader Group

Sign up for Ellie's Newsletter.
Elliemasters.com/newslettersignup

Military Romance

Guardian Hostage Rescue Specialists

Rescuing Melissa

(Get a FREE copy of Rescuing Melissa

when you join Ellie's Newsletter)

Alpha Team

Rescuing Zoe

Rescuing Moira

Rescuing Eve

Rescuing Lily

Rescuing Jinx

Rescuing Maria

Bravo Team

Rescuing Angie

Rescuing Isabelle

Rescuing Carmen

Rescuing Rosalie

Rescuing Kaye

Cara's Protector

Rescuing Barbi

Charlie Team

Rescuing Rebel

Rescuing Stitch

Rescuing Mia

Jenna's Protector

Rescuing Sophia

Rescuing Malia

Rescuing Ally

Delta Team (Coming Soon)

Rescuing Ember

Rescuing Aria

STANDALONES IN THE GUARDIAN HOSTAGE RESCUE SERIES YOU CAN READ ANYTIME

Military Romance

Guardian Personal Protection Specialists

Sybil's Protector

Lyra's Protector

Angel Peak Steamy Instalove Series

(Small Town Power Dynamics)

By Ellie Masters

EACH BOOK IN THIS SERIES CAN BE READ AS A STANDALONE AND IS ABOUT A DIFFERENT COUPLE WITH AN HEA.

SNOWED IN WITH THE MOUNTAIN DOCTOR

Rescued by the Mountain Guide

Stranded with the Resort Owner

Matched with the Small-Town Chef

Trapped with the Forest Ranger

Snowbound with the Vineyard Owner

Reunited with the Hometown Hero

Colliding with the Coffee Shop Owner

The One I Want Series

(Small Town, Military Heroes)

By Jet & Ellie Masters

Saving Abby

Saving Ariel

Saving Brie

Saving Cate

Saving Dani

Saving Jen

The LaRouge Triplets

Asher

Brody

Cage

Billionaire Romance

Billionaire Boys Club

Hawke

Richard

Contemporary Romance

Cocky Captain

Romantic Suspense

EACH BOOK IS A STANDALONE NOVEL.

The Starling

The Swan

~AND~

Science Fiction

Ellie Masters writing as L.A. Warren

Vendel Rising: a Science Fiction Serialized Novel

If you enjoyed this book by Ellie Masters, the LIGHTER SIDE of the Jet & Ellie writing duo, and aren't afraid of edgier writing, you might enjoy reading BDSM themed books written by Jet, the DARKER SIDE of the Masters' Writing Team.

The DARKER SIDE

Jet Masters is the darker side of the Jet & Ellie writing duo!

Romantic Suspense

Changing Roles Series:

THIS SERIES MUST BE READ IN ORDER.

Command Me

Control Me

Collar Me

Embracing FATE

Seizing FATE

Accepting FATE

HOT READS

A STANDALONE NOVEL.

Down the Rabbit Hole

Light BDSM Romance

The Ties that Bind

EACH BOOK IN THIS SERIES CAN BE READ AS A STANDALONE AND IS ABOUT A DIFFERENT COUPLE WITH AN HEA.

Alexa

Angel's Peak

Books by Jet Masters

If you enjoyed this book by Ellie Masters, the LIGHTER SIDE of the Jet & Ellie writing duo, and aren't afraid of edgier writing, you might enjoy reading BDSM themed books written by Jet, the DARKER SIDE of the Masters' Writing Team.

The DARKER SIDE
Jet Masters is the darker side of the Jet & Ellie writing duo!

Romantic Suspense
Changing Roles Series:
THIS SERIES MUST BE READ IN ORDER.
Command Me
Control Me
Collar Me
Embracing FATE
Seizing FATE
Accepting FATE

HOT READS

A STANDALONE NOVEL.
Down the Rabbit Hole

Light BDSM Romance
The Ties that Bind

EACH BOOK IN THIS SERIES CAN BE READ AS A STANDALONE AND IS ABOUT A DIFFERENT COUPLE WITH AN HEA.

Alexa
Penny
Michelle
Ivy

HOT READS
Becoming His Series

THIS SERIES MUST BE READ IN ORDER.
The Ballet
Learning to Breathe
Becoming His

Dark Captive Romance
A STANDALONE NOVEL.
She's MINE

About the Author

Ellie Masters is a USA Today Bestselling author and Amazon Top 15 Author who writes Angsty, Steamy, Heart-Stopping, Pulse-Pounding, Can't-Stop-Reading Romantic Suspense. In addition, she's a wife, military mom, doctor, and retired Colonel. She writes romantic suspense filled with all your sexy, swoon-worthy alpha men. Her writing will tug at your heart-strings and leave your heart racing.

Born in the South, raised under the Hawaiian sun, Ellie has traveled the globe while in service to her country. The love of her life, her amazing husband, is her number one fan and biggest supporter. And yes! He's read every word she's written.

She has lived all over the United States—east, west, north, south and central—but grew up under the Hawaiian sun. She's also been privileged to have lived overseas, experiencing other cultures and making lifelong friends. Now, Ellie is proud to call herself a Southern transplant, learning to say y'all and "bless her heart" with the best of them.

Ellie's favorite way to spend an evening is curled up on a couch, laptop in place, watching a fire, drinking a good wine, and bringing forth all the characters from her mind to the page and hopefully into the hearts of her readers.

FOR MORE INFORMATION
elliemasters.com

facebook.com/elliemastersromance

x.com/Ellie__Masters

instagram.com/ellie_masters

bookbub.com/authors/ellie-masters

goodreads.com/Ellie_Masters

Final Thoughts

I hope you enjoyed this book as much as I enjoyed writing it. If you enjoyed reading this story, please consider leaving a review on Amazon and Goodreads, and please let other people know. A sentence is all it takes. Friend recommendations are the strongest catalyst for readers' purchase decisions! And I'd love to be able to continue bringing the characters and stories from My-Mind-to-the-Page.

Second, call or e-mail a friend and tell them about this book. If you really want them to read it, gift it to them. If you prefer digital friends, please use the "Recommend" feature of Goodreads to spread the word.

Or visit my blog https://elliemasters.com, where you can find out more about my writing process and personal life.

Come visit The EDGE: Dark Discussions where we'll have a chance to talk about my works, their creation, and maybe what the future has in store for my writing.

Facebook Reader Group: Ellz Bellz

Thank you so much for your support!

Love,

Ellie

DEDICATION

This book is dedicated to you, my reader. Thank you for spending a few hours of your time with me. I wouldn't be able to write without you to cheer me on. Your wonderful words, your support, and your willingness to join me on this journey is a gift beyond measure.

Whether this is the first book of mine you've read, or if you've been with me since the very beginning, thank you for believing in me as I bring these characters 'from my mind to the page and into your hearts.'

Love,
Ellie

THE END

www.ingramcontent.com/pod-product-compliance
Lightning Source LLC
Chambersburg PA
CBHW031043310726
48969CB00007B/2097